Praise for THE STARS MUST WAIT

"An outstanding collection of stories, encompassing fantastic worlds and protagonists of immense complexity, subtlety and depth."

—Liz Williams, author of *Comet Weather* and The Inspector Chen series

"A collection of speculative fiction stories written by a gifted storyteller. The milieus are highly imaginative, the characters well-rounded and the narrative compelling. An absorbing and remarkable collection, I hope this book finds many readers."

—Teika Marija Smits, BFS Award winning author of *Umbilical* and *Waterlore*

THE STARS
MUST WAIT

CARMELO RAFALÀ

GUARDBRIDGE BOOKS
ST ANDREWS, SCOTLAND

Published by Guardbridge Books,
St Andrews, Fife, United Kingdom.

http://guardbridgebooks.co.uk

The Stars Must Wait

"Children of Itzamná" © 2019, 2025
"Heart of the City, Heart of the Sea" © 2020, 2025
"Slipping Sideways" © 2012, 20117, 2025
"Song for the Asking" © 2015, 2025
"The Clarity of Ice" © 2025
"The Roots of Love" © 2022, 2025
"The Stars Must Wait" © 2024, 2025
"What Happened to Mrs Eleonora Valdemar" © 2019, 2022, 2025

Edited by David Stokes

Cover art © Ben Baldwin

ISBN: 978-1-911486-98-5

CONTENTS

INTRODUCTION

Elana Gomel

Do you like stepping into a strange new world, alluring and mysterious, dazzling you with never-seen colours and dreamlike landscapes? Of course, you do, or you would not be reading fantasy. Then this collection is for you.

And do you like stories that make you think, that shatter your old assumptions and force you to consider familiar things from an unfamiliar perspective? Of course, you do, or you would not be reading science fiction. Then this collection is for you.

Are you one of those people who are curious about other cultures and other countries? Are you a traveller or a would-be traveller? Do you, perhaps, dream of the emerald jungles of Mesoamerica where cyclopean ruins and slinky jaguars remind us of the legacy of the Aztec and Maya civilizations? I will assume you are because I am. Then this collection is for both of us.

The first story in the collection sets the tone. "Song for the Asking" opens *in medias res*, with the first-person narrator penning increasingly urgent diary entries on board a mutinous ship that is taking him and his cargo to a distant

City. The cargo is an unconscious woman in a cage and a boy. You think you know where it is going, of course. You think the narrator is an evil slave trader, the mutineers are noble revolutionaries, and the boy and the woman are going to be set free, while the slaver gets his just comeuppance. Well, think again. Carmelo Rafalà does not give you easy answers nor pummel you with cartoon moralizing. He does not preach. He teaches.

By the end of the story, your assumptions will be turned upside down and you will learn something important about the power of faith that remakes a convert's identity, and about the hardship of being caught between two worlds. The protagonist's beautiful words speak to everyone who has exchanged the songs of their childhood for a different tune sung in a new language:

> And I know Abbot Diyari will be there, waiting,
>   that foreign man who instructs
>   me in strange ways and guides me with strange
> motives and calls me 'son'.
>   Sweet arpeggios, swift and bright—the
> language of my people, the people
>   of the Hinterlands—play within the breezes
> that come forward to touch my beaten
>   face and taunt my ears.
>   I rest my head into the wind, wishing I knew
> how to respond.

I loved this story because, like the author, I am a professional nomad and a cosmopolitan wanderer. But I also loved it because it is profound, unexpected, and beautifully written.

"Song for the Asking" is a fantasy, set in a Secondary World, whose outlines we glimpse only dimly (and I, for one, would like to know more). But other stories are SF or horror or both. Rafalà's imagination is both vivid and dark, creating settings and situations that are as relentlessly captivating as a nightmare.

The second story "Children of Itzamná" combines Mayan mythology (Itzamna is a Mayan creator god) with the glitter of futuristic tech and the brutality of cartel violence. It reminds me of Pat Murphy's *The Fallen Woman* and Arcady Martine's *The Memory Called Empire*. Written in the first person, like all the other stories in the collection, it has an unexpected protagonist and a twist you won't see coming. Ultimately, the story is about the unbroken strength of family bonds that transcend both the echoes of the violent past and the premonitions of the equally violent future.

The Science Fiction and Fantasy South Africa's Nova winning story, "The Stars Must Wait", is based on Yevgeny Zamyatin's dystopian novel *We* (1924), which Orwell acknowledged as the main inspiration for *Nineteen Eighty-Four*. It is hard to write tales set in somebody else's world, especially when the original is a classic, but Rafalà does it brilliantly. His story, set some decades after the end of *We*, amplifies the original's message while adapting it to our times when the utopian disillusionment of the past collides with the desire for a different future.

Zamyatin's novel was a prescient warning against the dangers of trying to create a perfect world, in which irrationality, violence, and greed would be stamped out by scientific algorithms. Rafalà's take on this shows that utopia remains a constant temptation, even though we know that a supposedly perfect society will inevitably devolve into violence against those who do not fit in:

> I watch the State burn, burn as K-121 did, burn like the house, with all its
> ancient, primaeval flotsam of philosophy and religion and free-thinking and
> selfish desires—the things that A-505 and his ilk admired. Everything burning.
> A mother. A child. Numbers and Mephi. The State and the natural world.
> Inside and Outside. Chaos and order. Reason and belief.

The other stories in the collection show the breadth and versatility of Rafalà's art. "The Roots of Love" and "What Happened to Mrs. Eleonora Valdemar, Discovered in a Series of Diary Entries" are two very different takes on the concept of revenge. The first story is a brief but intense horror tale about a woman transformed who exacts a bitter vengeance on her faithless lover. The second one is a historical horror and a crime mystery which allows us a glimpse into the increasingly unhinged mind of a nineteenth-century wife driven insane by her husband's abuse and neglect.

One of the connecting themes in the collection is that of love—between siblings, parents, friends, husbands and wives. Love offers no easy solutions, no "happily ever after". But it inspires courage and offers redemption, as in the deeply touching "Heart of the City, Heart of the Sea". In "Slipping Sideways", the SF concept of the multiverse is used to reflect upon the heartfelt regrets of a man who has destroyed his friends by a thoughtless love affair. Sweet and tender, the story suggests that we can still get second chances—if not in this life, then in another.

One of the most interesting aspects of the collection is that the same basic concepts are being explored through different genre mechanisms. "Heart of the City, Heart of the Sea" and "Slipping Sideways" are fantasy and SF versions of the same theme of redemption. In the last story, "The Clarity of Ice", SF conventions of terraforming, life in a space habitat, and creation of new life forms combine to generate a deeply human portrait of the struggling protagonist.

Rafalà's collection is one of the best single-author anthologies I have read in a long time. And having read it, I hope you will agree.

Elana Gomel
author, essayist, and academic

SONG FOR THE ASKING

Day 5

Mutiny is a swift predator: brutal, bloody, an entity without mercy.

We have been locked in the ship's hold for our own safety. From the decks above our heads, shouts, gunshots, and the sounds of running echoed down the stairwells and airshafts to pummel the steel door that keeps us alive.

Me.

The boy.

The woman in the cage.

When the bloodshed is over, we are let out and assemble on deck with the remaining crew. A few men, hand-picked by Master Hautalo, stand with weapons drawn.

The bodies of the dead are wrapped in white sheets and carried upon shoulders. As a Brother of the Church of the Everlasting, I am asked to say prayers over the departed, and one by one the dead crewmen are dropped into the sea.

The few who remain loyal to the captain sit in one of the skiffs, now hanging over the ship's side. Hautalo speaks to them in a low, steady voice, then steps back while Jenko and a crewman named Marl, a plump and red-cheeked Northern man, lower the craft into the water. Oars in hands, the men push themselves away.

Their chances on the open sea are slim.

Out here.

Where the raiders of Estua-Nin roam.

I offer the men a silent prayer while I watch them rowing towards certain death.

The boy is looking up at the cargo crane, mouth open, face ashen. Tied high upon the beam is the captain's bloodied corpse. It is a sign of his shame—and Hautalo's newfound authority.

"Avert your eyes, my son," I tell him.

He bows his head without a word.

*

I take the boy back near the stern, behind the bridge tower, where the deep thumping of the engines vibrates through the deck like a heartbeat. He does not look at me but continues to stare down at the decking. I can sense his fear, and I squeeze his arm gently.

Deck gunners are sitting at their weapons, scanning the horizon. And holding positions behind us are the five remaining sister ships of what once was a convoy of nine.

Hautalo follows us back and slumps against a deck gun, chewing his cigar, considering us.

I do my best to remain impassive. "Is there a problem?"

His cigar smoulders between his lips. He looks haggard, but his eyes, bloodshot as they are, are alive with suspicion.

"You know there is."

"I paid for transportation, *and* privacy," I say. "All in advance. Your former captain accepted."

"For you, a boy and a woman."

"And that is what you have."

"What I have is a woman under a blanket in a covered cage, Brother Sunde. Unlike our former captain, I want to know why."

"Suddenly, a merchant takes issue with the type of cargo he ferries across the deeper sea. How strange."

"Well, Brother Sunde?"

"So, you are a moral man, are you?"

He folds his arms across his chest. "Brother, we've lost three ships and our fair share of comrades. Our captain was not prepared to do what was necessary to protect the men. I am."

His subtle threat makes me perspire. I try not to fidget with my robes.

"Her semiconscious state is meditative," I say, "self-induced, not chemical. She is processing. Normal after periods of heavy tuition."

He nods. "A seminarian."

"Yes," I say.

The boy looks up at me, his face tinged with unease.

Hautalo eyes the boy, then me. He chews his cigar some more. "So, you are saying the cage is for her protection from the men?"

"Yes. Appropriate enough, considering her condition and our long journey."

He holds up our documents. "Your papers could be forgeries."

"Are you suggesting I'm a slave trader?"

"You're not Cityfolk."

My ears burn with the offence. "You are addressing a Brother of the Church of the Everlasting, and I serve the Abbot of Rik-Tarshin with the utmost devotion."

"Devotion." He turns the word over in his mouth several times. "A Hinterland convert. Many of you would sell your own daughters if the price was right. Many have done so."

"If you are as brave as you are bold, I can arrange an audience with the abbot upon our arrival," I say. "You may take up any of your meaningless reservations with him."

Hautalo seems to be deliberating again, then flicks the cigar overboard.

"Very well, *Brother* Sunde, I will take you at your word."

"You will honour the terms of our original agreement?"

"Yes."

I thank him and prod the boy to do the same.

Hautalo scowls. "Remember, Brother Sunde, that as long as Estua-Nin's raiders infest these waters I cannot guarantee your safety."

"The conflicts between the city-states of this region are not my mission. We must be in Rik-Tarshin in seventeen days."

"Seventeen days, *if* the raiders allow it." He calls out to the new first mate, "Jenko!"

The new first mate is standing near, slicing a piece of apple away from its core with a long knife. He tosses the rest of the fruit overboard and replaces the blade in the sheath on his boot. "Aye, sir."

"Prepare to get under way."

Deck gunners prime their weapons. There is the click of artillery shells locking into place.

"You know, Brother," says Hautalo, "if we are boarded,

I doubt that cage would stop a determined man. I take no responsibility for her. Or the boy." He walks off.

The boy utters a deep trilling sound. He does this when confused or frightened. He does not understand the sounds of our common language any more than I do. But at least he can make these few sounds. I was taken far too young to remember how.

The breeze tugs at my cassock. Pulling my robes about me, I glance at the darkening sky. The wind does not carry whispers now; there is no song in its currents, only a deep hissing.

"The past is a dead heart, my son," I say. "We make the sounds of Citymen now."

"Forgive me." His voice shakes.

I place my hand on his shoulder. "Faith teaches us strength. And how do we approach faith?"

"Trust in the church."

"And?"

"Fealty."

"These bring us peace of mind." I pinch his arm gently. "You would do well to remember your catechism."

Despite his lapses, he is a dedicated boy, eager to please. More than what he had been when the authorities in Faulk brought him to me—a street urchin, an orphan of the Hinterlands, living hand-to-mouth like an animal. Much like I once did, before Abbot Diyari took me in.

I want to encourage the boy, to guide him with a gentler hand than I ever knew. I bristle at the memory of my tuition, and the scars of penance that still live in deep pink lines across my torso.

"What's wrong, Brother?" The boy is peering at my face.

I've been staring at him, and my eyes are filled with tears. "Nothing. Just tired, that's all."

He stands, gazing up at me, pondering my answer. I tousle his hair, and he smiles. It makes my heart sing to know that soon, when he completes his first catechism, I will give him a name, just as Abbot Diyari had named me.

He casts his gaze to the hatch which leads down to the hold of the ship, and the caged woman waiting below. That strange woman who does not speak or cry out in her pain.

It is forbidden to give a Cityman's name to a nonbeliever, to someone who has not passed through catechism. The boy will earn his name, but I feel she must have an identity, as well. Secretly, I call her Rydra.

"What we bring the abbot is a great prize," I say. "The faithful will read about what we've done for ages to come."

He says nothing but leans closer to me, as though true comfort resides not only in my words but in my close physical presence. Like a son to a father.

*

…many mornings I would stand at the back of the great hall in Rik-Tarshin to watch the faithful crowd into the sanctuary, watch closely those who would hope to touch a scrap of the robes of Theosis, the First Abbot, and acquire wisdom. For a small tithe, some are granted an audience with the Skulls of the Sacred—remnants of the first, great Citymen—in the hope of obtaining vitality.

I was envious that the abbot had been brought such wonders of the ancient world by brothers who had proved their devotion. And they had been rewarded in various ways, as true sons would by a proud father.

And so forsaking comfort and all aid—and with the blessing of the Council—I left the cathedral, and Rik-Tarshin, and set out on the Pilgrimage.

I walked the deserts and prairies of the Hinterlands, suffered many hardships, lived frugally, and prayed relentlessly.

But I never found any holy relics…

Day 6

Rydra spends most of her time sleeping. During her semi-conscious moments, I feed her bread dipped in condensed milk. Sometimes, she gazes out through half-opened eyes, irises the colour of desert sand.

I pull back the blanket ever so slightly (and true to his tuition, the boy turns away and does not look upon her exposed flesh). The gas lamp suspended above highlights a network of cuts and bruises. Her skin is pale, ghostly. Her hair, as white and as clean as fresh linen, flows softly about her shoulders.

Without turning his head, the boy hands me a cloth dabbed with ointment. As I clean her arms the boy begins to chant the Creed of Theosis. I listen carefully as I work. When he is finished, I smile with satisfaction. He's remembered every line. Every word.

When I reach behind Rydra, I brush the grazes there, careful to avoid the two distinct folds of skin that run the length of her back on either side of her spine. They look like layers of calluses, folded in on each other. The wounds bleed a little as the scabs come free.

I don't know where she was found, or how she came to be in a slaver's market, but I understand for what purpose she would've been sold.

I first set eyes upon the woman while travelling back to my parish in Faulk. Taking a short route through the valley, I passed through the town of Mordia. The slave market bustled and stank of blood and faeces; slavers shouted above the din.

And there she was, what I believed was a Hinterland woman, lying on a slaver's cart, naked, unmoving, bruised body chained to the wooden flatbed, wrists bound. Her breathing was so shallow I'd almost mistaken her for dead.

Something stirred within me, a deep pain I had not known before. I hadn't thought of my mother since being sent away to Faulk, but I thought of her at that moment: a slight woman, with flowing yellow hair and a smile like rays of sun.

What I did next shocked me. I took my leather purse, pregnant with the tithes of desperate believers, and dropped that hefty bag of coins at the slaver's feet.

It was only later that I came to recognize the type of bind that tied her wrists together: numinous cords from ancient days, fashioned by the first Citymen to bring low the people of cloud and air and secure them to the earth.

Our ancestors.

And she lay before me, a strange, eldritch remnant of those from which we Hinterlanders are descendants...

As I finish cleaning her wounds, I am struck by a sudden awareness.

She is awake.

Sitting back on my haunches I stare down at her face—her ethereally beautiful face. She is looking beyond me, to the boy. She tries to raise herself on one elbow, then flops back upon the cage floor.

"It's time, my son," I say.

The boy sighs heavily, then passes back to me a small ceramic demitasse. After taking a small bottle from my satchel, I pour out the correct amount of sedative. As I bring the cup to her lips she turns her head, and her whole body convulses violently. I pull back, spilling drops of the sedative on my robes.

"Brother…" The boy wants to turn around.

"Stay as you are."

Her chest heaves, and she pushes herself into a seated position. Swaying like a drunkard, she holds out her bound wrists to me.

Can she see the fear in my face? I cannot tell. Her expression is unreadable.

She collapses to the floor again.

Hands shaking, I pick up the sedative bottle and pour out another measure.

The boy, back still turned, has become anxious and whimpers something, some tonal phrasing.

The woman looks at him and puffs air from her mouth, a series of subtle breathy sounds, as if trying to respond.

Day 9

We lost another ship during the night.

In the morning the cramped mess hall heaves with

boatmen lining up for breakfast. The men do not speak. Silence lives between them, a reflective, solemn quiet.

Once we've received our bowls, I lead the boy to a long table, where Hautalo sits at its head. He motions at a place near his end, and I sit, the boy squeezing in next to me.

I ask about the missing ship, the *Sea Dawn*.

Hautalo chews his food but does not look up. "Brother Sunde, if our aid would've changed the situation, I would've ordered it so. That ship was hit hard with concentrated weapons fire. A generator was knocked out, the engines were a hopeless pile of scrap, and they were bleeding fuel."

"What of the men on that ship?"

Hautalo looks into his bowl. "I gave the order to cut loose."

"You mean you fled?"

The men stiffen, spoons frozen in mid-air.

Hautalo fixes me with an icy glare. "And what would you have me do, Brother Sunde, with these simple cargo carriers? Attack raiders? Survival is the first order."

"Captain never would've left comrades behind," says a man named Crist.

A few men mutter among themselves.

Hautalo points his spoon at the man. "You are here, mister, for one obvious reason: lack of space in the skiff. You would do well to keep that in mind."

"And I am grateful you spared my life by allowing me to remain aboard," says Crist, "but he *was* our captain. By *law*. His brother died on one of the ships we lost. He was mad with grief. If given more time we could've talked him down. He was almost ready to listen."

"Almost is too late," says Hautalo. "We needed to act. And I will not waste any more time explaining that simple fact to you."

There are voices of agreement, prodded along by Jenko's agitations.

The boy speaks. "But you have bigger ships. Theirs are small."

"And built for speed," says Hautalo. "We cannot outrun them."

The boy nods, slowly.

"Ships that small need a supply chain way out here, boy," says Jenko. "Our former captain said he knew of a depot in this region, at the Uvalu Atoll. He wanted to storm it, break the chain."

"And these men are merchants, you see, boy," Hautalo adds, "not military."

"'Tis true, dat is," says Marl, the fat Northern man.

Other men raise their voices in agreement.

"You are men of Rik-Tarshin," I say. "Appeal to the Council. They will provide you escorts."

Crist scoffs. "Just like that, hey? You've been away a *long* time, Brother Sunde."

"And this conversation is over." Hautalo glares at him.

Crist thrusts his spoon into his bowl, stirring its contents violently. "The abbots once raised armies to subdue the new lands, and to apply and uphold the law among Citymen—"

"Crist."

"—and what do they do now? Collect remnants of ancient days to remind themselves of how impressive they once were. And while they brood on past glory, the world they built collapses upon itself."

Hautalo slams his fist on the table. The boy flinches, and I place my hand upon his leg, to calm him.

"Master Jenko," he says, "take this man into custody. Assemble the crew on deck in one hour to watch Crist receive punishment for insubordination."

"Aye, sir." Jenko rises from his chair, hand on his holstered weapon.

Crist glares at Hautalo across the table, then slowly puts his spoon down and gets up. Jenko escorts him from the room.

Some men exchange hard glances, while others continue eating, deliberately, cautiously, as though waiting for something. Utensils scrape bowls. The ship gently rocks. No one utters a word. It remains like this for some time.

It is the boy's voice, soft and melodic, that first breaks the silence. "The raiders. How many are there?"

"If we are vigilant," says Hautalo, "and disciplined, we shall make it through."

"Not ta worry, lad," says Marl. "Da Brother will pray ta da Everlastin' for us. Maybe dose raider bullets will simply pass urs by."

Some of the men snicker.

I clear my throat. "I am always happy to offer prayer, individually or corporately."

"See here," says the fat crewman. "Ya really want ta offer sometin', why don't ya rouse dat girlie ta give urs a dance."

The men, seemingly revived by the jolly spirit of this

fat man, whoop, and clank their spoons to the sides of their tin bowls.

"The seminarian never dances," says the boy, indignant. He looks at me. "She processes."

"Ah!" The fat boatman chuckles. "Well, ya think, Captain Hautalo, ya can give me permission ta go down dar? I got some of me own processin' I'd like ta do."

The men roar with laughter.

"Take no notice of our bloated comrade, boy." Hautalo leans forward. "After pulling a double shift and enjoying half-rations tonight, Marl is going to scrub the sanitary closets."

The men jeer loudly at the fat boatman and bang their fists on the table.

Day 11

The wail of the siren penetrates through the body of the great ship, all the way down into the hold. Guns rumble overhead. A muffled explosion makes the vessel shudder.

The boy looks uneasy, as he did in the early days of our journey before he found his sea legs.

I'm pouring out a measure of sedative when Rydra utters a discordant note. I drop the cup and throw myself back against the bars of the cage.

"She speaks!" I whisper. "By the Everlasting, she speaks."

Another explosion, this one nearer and louder. The ship rocks violently, and the boy cries out in a shrill voice. It is the sound of fear.

Rydra reacts to the boy, calls to him in a long, drawn-out wail, a sound so lamentable gooseflesh rises on my arms.

The boy cocks his head and wraps both arms around his chest. He is terrified, of her, the guns, or both. In this mad rushing moment, I cannot tell.

The ship pitches to one side. I grab hold of the bars to remain upright. The boy falls sideways, howling as he hits the deck.

And Rydra replies—it is a riotous screeching, like a bow dragged across the strings of a violin. It's so loud and terrible the noise almost deafens me as it slices through my head. The boy claps his hands over his ears.

She does this several times until she falls unconscious again.

Day 12

"All right," says Hautalo. "I want to know who you *really* are, and what the hell you've brought aboard my ship."

Wisps of black smoke roll across the deck in slow, phantom motions, strangely illuminated by the orange and gold of the morning sun. A ship, the *Marigold*, is badly damaged and sits close to our port side.

When everything calmed, Hautalo's armed men stormed the hold and dragged us all topside. The armed men now keep their distance, weapons cradled in their arms. Crist and the gunners stand at their posts, frozen with uncertainty.

"I am Brother Sunde," I say. "From Faulk."

"And this is a seminarian?" He points to the woman

lying unconscious on the deck. He covers her with his long coat.

Jenko is leaning forward, as though about to step out of his overcoat. By his side is the boy, on one knee. He has the child gripped firmly by the arm.

The boy appeals to me with his eyes. I hold up my hand to him and make the sign of faith.

"Bother Sunde," says Hautalo, "I will not ask you again—"

"I am who I say I am. The abbot will vouch for me."

"And who will vouch for her?" Jenko lets the boy go, who rushes to me, grips my robes, and sobs quietly.

"What creature makes a sound like that?" says Hautalo. "A sound to freeze the spirit and send men running?"

"Not exactly a seminarian, is she?" says Jenko.

Like the boy, I, too, am frozen with fear.

"Brother Sunde," Hautalo continues, "we had twelve raider ships bearing down on us. *Twelve.* And when they heard that sound—and it was *heard*, as though it thundered from the very air around us—they turned and *fled.*"

"I didn't know. I didn't know," I babble. "Didn't know that she could speak. I thought her mute."

"*Brother,*" says Hautalo, the very tone of his voice is a threat.

I try to compose myself. "I...am a Brother of the Church. And she is...and she...is—"

"Syrmulus," Jenko says the ancient word, ancient in the tongue of Citymen.

The crewmen speak in terrified whispers.

"One of the elemental peoples of the Hinterlands,"

Crist says wildly, "brought low, kept in a cage; ancient from the time of the first Citymen—"

"A few could've escaped the purges," Jenko says.

Crist's face is sick with fear. "This is what you bring the abbot? *This?*"

Crewmen shout, "Kill it! Kill it!"

Panic overtakes me. "No! Those binds are holy and will keep her grounded. We are in no danger." I look to Hautalo. "I thought she was mute."

The men shuffle their feet. Fear is etched in every weather-beaten line of the men's faces. Hautalo sees it, too, and signals his armed men. They move among the crew cautiously, gripping their weapons as they go.

"It is foolhardy to keep her on board," says Crist. "You must get rid of her."

"Shut up!" Hautalo snaps.

Marl bounds through the hatch and onto the deck. He rushes to Jenko, places on object in his hands, and speaks in a low voice.

Jenko looks at it, then holds the sedative bottle up for all to see. "I suppose, Brother Sunde, she is quite passive, quiet. At least for the time being. Yes?"

I nod slowly.

Hautalo and Jenko exchange knowing glances. I look from one to the other, searching their faces.

"The boy," Hautalo says to me. "You said he cried out, and that's when she began to speak."

"Yes."

"I see." Hautalo casts his gaze out to the still morning waters. "Jenko, call the bridge. I want to know how far we've travelled from the Uvalu Atoll."

Jenko hands him the bottle and moves to the intercom.

"Marl," says Hautalo. "Put the boy in my cabin. Secure him there."

I pull the child closer to me and hug him fiercely. The burning in my lungs reminds me to breathe. "Whatever your intentions I beg you, keep the boy out of it."

Crist's face is pale. "You think you can control a creature like that, Captain?"

"Our passengers can," he says. "They've been doing it for weeks." He twists the bottle between his fingers. "With *this*."

"I didn't know she could speak," I protest. "And the boy doesn't understand—"

Marl pulls the boy from me. The child struggles and begins to squawk. Hautalo steps over and grips his jaw.

"No talking," he says, "until I say so. You wouldn't want anything" —he pulls out his gun and points it at the woman's head— "*unfortunate* to happen to the woman."

The boy looks to me for help, tears streaming from his beautiful eyes. I want to speak words of comfort to him, but they fail to come from my mouth.

The boy's shoulders droop forward, and he hangs his head, breath sporadic through quiet sobs. He allows himself to be led below.

My stomach twists. "Captain, I implore you. Honour our agreement. *Please*."

"Medic!"

A small man comes forward.

"The woman goes back to her cage. And take care of this." He hands over the sedative. "It's vital the drug is administered at the correct times. Brother Sunde will...*assist* you."

The medic calls to another man, and together they lift her gently from the deck, and carry her to the hatch.

Jenko returns. "The Atoll is eight days away, north-by-northwest. Six days at full speed. Fuel reserves are fine. We can do it."

"Signal the *Marigold*. She is to continue her course away from here," he says. "The *Venture* will be her escort and provide cover. Inform the *Daystar* and *Azoria* to remain with us. We're going back."

"Back!" Crist says. "Hautalo. *Captain*. You are deceived."

Hautalo sneers. "What's the matter, Crist? You fought with our former captain against the raiders. Now suddenly you don't have the belly for it?"

The armed men chuckle at this; the crew smile nervously and grip their belts.

Crist sidles up to Hautalo. "You'll still have an inquest to face *if* we make landfall. Don't forget that. I won't."

Hautalo considers him for only a moment, then breaks the man's nose.

Day 17

I am not allowed to be alone with Rydra. An armed guard stays with me in the hold. When he is needed to attend to other duties, I am locked in a sanitary closet.

In her semiconscious state, Rydra makes no sound but stares with empty eyes at the spot where the boy used to sleep. She keeps her back to me.

I finish administering balms to Rydra's wounds and

close and lock the door to her cage. The medic takes from me the key, the sedative, the salves, and the cloth and puts them in my satchel. He slings the bag over his shoulder and leaves.

The guard snaps to attention.

Hautalo is standing in the doorway.

The guard greets the captain with a salute.

"He salutes you," I say. "So, this is a military operation now?"

Hautalo rolls a cigar between his teeth.

"I want to see the boy," I say.

He sucks hard and blows out a puff of thick, white smoke.

I should choose my words carefully, but the affront to my person chokes me with indignation. "I cannot, in good conscience, be a willing part of this, nor can I allow—"

"Good conscience?" Hautalo takes slow, deliberate strides toward me. "You hardly have the moral high ground here." He points a finger at Rydra. "You came aboard under false pretences and talk to me of good conscience?"

I feel my cheeks flush. "I merely withheld information. For a very good reason."

"You people have no good reasons for anything you do. I said you're not Cityfolk, didn't I?"

I'm consumed by both my failings in these matters and my resentment that he could so callously dismiss me.

"I am Brother Sunde—"

"—of the Church of the Everlasting," he spits out. "So you've said."

"Raised in the Rectory at Rik-Tarshin! Instructed by Abbot Diyari *himself*—"

"—but still not a Cityman."

"—and I will not allow you—" I swallow my next words, for I know how hollow they will sound.

Hautalo leans casually against the doorframe. I seem to amuse him.

"A Hinterland convert." He shakes his head. "Who heads a mission in Faulk. *Faulk*. Not exactly a place of inspiration. But you've done one good deed, convert, though unintentionally. You've created for me an incredible opportunity, and with that woman's assistance—"

"You took command to save the men. I understand that..."

He grunts. "I'm still going to save the men. And many more. We're heading for the Atoll. No doubt it will be heavily guarded, but that may no longer be a problem for us. If you want to survive this and take back your trophy to the abbot, you'll cooperate. You don't have a choice in the matter."

"Captain Hautalo, *please*. For the love of the Everlasting, don't do this. Stop this madness!"

"Yes," he says, "for the love of the Everlasting, I will stop this madness."

He shuts and bolts the door.

*

I've never overseen mass conversions to the faith, nor contributed to the sacred history of the church through Pilgrimage. I've been assaulted by my Hinterland brethren on more than one occasion, endured a volley of stones, and fled a mob under cover of darkness to a neighbouring village—shameful incidences which had me recalled to the Rectory to give an account of myself.

Considering my many difficulties, Abbot Diyari decided it best to send me away to Faulk.

I begged him to reconsider. Faulk is a small community: safe, reliable in its meagre but steady support, conservative, and uninteresting.

He told me our talents and our appointments must not be mutually exclusive; that they must complement each other.

I resisted and declared there was so much more I wanted to do, so much more I could do. For the church. For him.

He told me, yes, yes there was.

And I would do it in Faulk.

Day 19

The ship's portside guns thunder into the day's dying light. Raider ships are there, black needles cutting through the water, advancing upon our convoy at great speed.

The medic helps me guide Rydra up on deck, and we are escorted by two guards. She struggles against us. The sedative is wearing off, but the ancient binds around her wrists are secure, and she cannot break them. Jenko is there, holding the port railing as the ship rises and falls. A storm is brewing, and a thin rain sprays our faces.

The *Daystar* and the *Azoria* begin fanning out, forcing the enemy line to fracture. A group of raider ships break away and head straight for us.

Jenko signals a crewman, who disappears into a hatch. The boy is brought on deck, struggling in Marl's clutches.

"What are you doing?" I say, cradling Rydra with one arm.

Jenko waves to the men, who haul the boy across the deck and tie him to the cargo crane. Marl works a lever and the arm rises. The boy dangles there, howling discordant notes.

The horror of perception grips me. They're putting the boy in peril, forcing him to cry out, as he'd done before, to rouse her monstrous voice.

The elemental woman.

The boy. My boy.

"Jenko, no!"

Rydra, eyes half open, turns her head to the boy. She twists in an attempt to break free of the medic's grip and he stumbles and crashes into the railing, taking me and Rydra with him.

The raiders are closing on us. Sporadic gunfire lights up the night, and the *Azoria* is on fire.

A speaker crackles and Hautalo's voice booms through the air, *"Target atoll, dead ahead. All hands ready. We're going to make a break for it."*

I can just make out Hautalo at the bridge window. He turns to speak to the helmsman, and the engines increase their pounding. We pick up speed, pulling ahead of the other two carriers.

I begin to tremble, not just my hands or legs, but my entire body. I feel as if I am suffocating. I see my prize slip away, a revered place among my honoured Brothers denied, and the proud father turning his back on me, as he did all those years ago.

I stare at the boy, and a cold, slow fear drips down my body and trickles over my scars.

I cry out, "*Give me my son!*"

Jenko signals Marl, who turns the wheel, and the crane arm rotates and swings out over the sea. The boy's panic-stricken song pierces through the crashing of waves.

Rydra convulses and looks up, eyes now wide. And from her throat comes a terrible sound: deep, dissonant, like a church organ growling.

Jenko comes over, one hand resting on the pistol holstered at his side. The medic's face is a sheet of white. "I'll take her." Jenko reaches out and grips Rydra's arm. The medic moves back to stand with the guards.

Jenko shakes her with fury. "Come on, you monster. You can do better than *that*."

Swallowing the bile in my throat, I gather my courage and shove my elbow into Jenko's face. He lets go of Rydra and stumbles back; the woman wobbles and falls over, and I let her weight take me with her. Before Jenko can act, I reach out, snatch the long blade from the sheath on his boot, and cut the holy bindings around her wrists.

Now free, she loses the pallor of her nakedness, and her body changes, becomes less substantial, almost translucent, as though she is but a wisp of illuminated cloud. She draws herself up to her full height; the soft features of her face alter, and she is something altogether different, a creature both beautiful and terrifying.

In one swift motion, Rydra extends her arms at the elbows and flexes her fingers. From her body comes a great swooshing sound, as though a gas primer had just been lit. A wall of air, only visible by its trail across the water, speeds outward to shatter the advancing raider ships into kindling.

Gunners abandon their posts and run for the deck house, mid-ship. Jenko sways between rage and horror. He pulls out his pistol, but I spring up to block his aim. Knife still in my hand, he must assume I'm trying to kill him. There is a popping noise, and my shoulder explodes with fire. The vessel heaves up under me, and my face hits the cold, wet deck.

A scream. I look up just in time to see Jenko and the armed guards being flung overboard in a gust of wind. Three more armed men stumble forward and raise their weapons. Rydra emits one discordant sound, a grinding of notes, and the men are hurled against the deck house bulkhead. Cracked skulls smear red and grey across white paint.

Hautalo is scrambling down the stairs of the bridge tower, rifle in hand. He stops, lets off a warning shot into the air, and continues down.

Rydra ignores him, and me, and moves towards the crane and the boy, still hanging over the sea, crying and wailing. Marl has no chance. With a flex of her fingers, Rydra sends him flying into the storm.

"*Stop!*" Hautalo runs ahead of her and lets off another shot. She halts and looks at him, eyes slits. He begins to walk backwards, slowly, towards the crane controls. Working the crane's wheel, he swings the boy back over the deck. The child hangs there, crying in fractured arpeggios.

I pull myself to my knees. The sleeve of my robe is heavy with warm blood. Pain travels in waves down my arm.

The sea near us is full of debris and dead bodies, and the other raider groups are concentrating on our sister ships in the distance behind us. The *Daystar* is taking heavy fire. The *Azoria* is listing, and in minutes, she will sink.

Hautalo remains where he stands, rifle in hand.

Rydra's throat grumbles with dark tones.

"Captain," I say into the rain. "I'm sorry…"

His face is pregnant with loathing. "You filthy Hinterland son of a bitch!"

I hear the rifle cock.

The creases on either side of Rydra's spine ripple. In a motion as rapid and as fluid as a bird's she extends great wings, thin membranes that glow with a silver-white light.

I swallow a deep helping of air, like an infant taking its first breath of life. If terror has gripped Hautalo he doesn't show it.

Hautalo is no fool. He knows the convoy is lost. His hope has died, along with all the souls he's needlessly committed to the deep. There is nothing he can do now, except, maybe, flee the area, and if we make it home, face an inquest for murder and mutiny. But that is not his way. He will follow another course.

"I should kill you, Sunde!"

He raises the rifle, but he aims it at the boy.

Rydra rushes him with inhuman speed and lifts him into the air. The gun goes off—a shot into the darkness.

They hover above the ship for only a few seconds, then she pulls him into the sky with her, into the whirling tempest, wings flapping furiously.

His screams are lost in a cacophony of cyclonic arpeggios.

Day 31

A gull cries somewhere overhead, and the smell of land is in the air. Our vessel limps toward the dock at Rik-Tarshin, bleeding smoke, engines emitting a sickly groan.

My shoulder still aches. The medic could not remove the bullet, but at least he had stopped the bleeding...

Crist is in command now, the man with the broken nose who stood by one doomed captain and stood up against another.

And we've received no word of the *Marigold*, or the *Venture*.

What of Rydra? She is free, as free as our people once were...

After days of anxious sailing, we met up with another convoy. Together, we made landfall only once, at a small port town whose name escapes me. A few crewmen got off. The boy went with them, the boy I'd cared for, and nurtured. The boy I'd hoped, one day, would be a seminarian, a scholar of the faith, and ordained as a Brother. The son of a proud father.

I hang high above the deck now, tied to the cargo crane. As the ship nears the dock, I cannot cast my gaze upon the Rectory, which stands tall and proud on a hillside, but I can almost feel its heavy shadow reaching out to me.

And Abbot Diyari will be there, waiting, that foreign man who instructs me in strange ways and guides me with strange motives and calls me 'son'.

Sweet arpeggios, swift and bright—the language of my people, the people of the Hinterlands—play within the breezes that come forward to touch my beaten face and taunt my ears.

I rest my head into the wind, wishing I knew how to respond.

CHILDREN OF ITZAMNÁ

After the war, the flesh traders came.
Low-grade tech-dealers responded by setting up stalls in villages and towns, making personality backups of the little children and selling them in jewellery to frightened parents for a modest fee.
Those who could not afford a backup begged on their knees. Mothers bawled 'Save my babies!' while angry fathers beat their chests and pulled their hair...
—Jorge Ortega
Aftermath

I.

Our automated limo came to a stop at the last security zone.

"Now play the part, Malinal," I said, casually running my fingers down the front of my strapless bodice. "That's all you have to do. Stay calm. No smart mouthing. Don't look me in the eyes, sit straight, shoulders back. Remain a step behind me and no assertive posturing; it's a dead giveaway when your chupacabra begins to growl."

Malinal glowered at me. "I'm thirteen, Papan, but I'm not stupid."

She turned away and I knew she caught a glimpse of herself reflected in the glass. A tremor of revulsion passed through her at the sight of her own luminous blue eyes, the sheen of her perfect bronze skin shimmering in the Yucatán sun, and the elaborate coloured swirling patterns stitched into and carved across her transformed body.

She was a Painted One, and as a child of the cenote blood-waters, reborn, she could be anything one wanted: a servant, a toy, an object of perversion.

Like Jago was.

Like you were, Adalia…

Images invaded my memory, of us playing on the Tulum beaches, collecting shells, building palaces of sand, and letting the waves dance at our feet. Happier times.

Pain pulsed behind my eyes, and I reached up to stroke my temples with both index fingers. Malinal watched me with a pensive, curious look.

"I never said you were stupid, Malinal," I said. "Anyone who can hack into a *Bastard* data-node and extract such detailed information is not stupid. But you need discipline."

"You keep saying that."

"These are the *Bastards of Magdeleine*. Mérida is their city. You don't simply walk into their midst and kidnap merchandise."

She swallowed hard. "You said you could do it!" Her chupacabra stirred, wrapped its furry arms around her waist, and chattered furiously at her sudden outburst. The lemur-sized creature flexed its spinal quills and clung to her possessively, looking out at me with large, dark eyes.

Chupacabras and aggression don't mix. I'd once witnessed this fact at a party when one of those creatures demonstrated its aversion to belligerence by rearing up and chewing the face off of its pubescent owner. The poor kid hadn't settled well into his new identity. I only hoped his parents had paid for a backup.

"Getting your brother's living body back depends on you," I said. "Are you going to act like my merchandise?"

Fear settled on her. I could smell it. She was no longer the brassy girl who'd strode up to me in Motul, as yet unchanged by the blood-waters, demanding my services, paying my full fee upfront, monies ripped from personal accounts with shitty firewalls and uninspired passwords. Find her brother's living, painted body, that was the job, free him from captivity...

"Either we do this right, Malinal, or we walk away. There's always a choice."

"You keep saying that as well." She breathed deeply and clutched at her chest, feeling for the pendant—Jago's backup. Malinal's father had given it to her, she'd said, before putting a gun in his mouth.

Jaog's backup was last updated two weeks before he was stolen, so he would remember nothing of his kidnapping, or what he endured after that. But Malinal could never return his colourful and twisted body to its original form any more than she could change her own. As a result, I would need to take them both to Colombia and the relative safety of South America and for that, it would cost her extra.

I always honour my arrangements, but if truth be told, Adalia, it was going to be difficult to see that one through...

Malinal squeezed the pendant hard, knuckles white. When she opened her hand, an impression lay etched on her palm: Itzamná, ruler of heaven and healing.

I looked to the sky, to the Bondi Platform hanging above the city. Up there that fat man Zorislav Durakovic, an influential businessman from Sarajevo and patron of the city's Carnival, would dine with his intimates for five days and nights.

The circumstances were perfect. All I needed was for Malinal to work with me. If she didn't fall apart at the slightest sign of pressure, I might pull this off—

I brushed my belt with my hands—a scattering field that concealed the gun strapped to my inner thigh from the prying electronics of the security checkpoints. My elaborate dress hid the more traditional, non-technical weapons in its adornments.

I thought of you, Adalia. A pang of guilt gripped my heart. Malinal might just see Jago again. But I'd never get you back, beloved sister. We'd never be a family again.

Four armed soldiers moved toward our car.

"Okay." I leaned forward. "This is the final security check. We do this as rehearsed, or these guys will kill us right here."

A soldier's gloved hand knocked on the window.

*

The security office was a small, damp room: one tinted window, paint peeling off the concrete, and minimal lighting. Somewhere in the walls, a lavatory pipe was leaking. The room smelled of piss.

Outside was a large clearing about half a mile in diameter, ringed by desolate buildings, which stood like battered sentinels. The Platform, now stationary, took up a sizable chunk of sky. Directly beneath, four plasti-glass elevation pods stood waiting to carry up passengers on taut steel cables.

"We have one computer servicing this entire tower," said the man across the desk. "It could be an hour or more."

"Unacceptable!" I sat, solid as ice, hands clasped together as if in prayer. "Do you even know who you're speaking to?"

"A Daughter of the Minor House of Majahual," said the man, sweating. "But I have no record of your entrance to Motul; no record of you crossing the border from Quintana Roo, so—if you'll forgive me—I need to run a check—"

From my clasped hands I launched two golden spikes into his brain. His eyes burst inward, his head whipped back, and blood poured out of his eye holes, down his cheeks. His white shirt caught the flow, soaking up the crimson.

Malinal retched and hugged her chupacabra close, and the creature nuzzled her and cooed.

I leapt from my chair and, taking the man's forefinger, pushed his fingerprint onto the screen in a box marked 'Approved'; then I hit 'enter'.

At the far end of the room was a disused elevator. Having studied the layout of this building, I knew it led underground to what had once been a parking garage for employees. I forced open the door, dumped his body down the empty shaft, and turned to Malinal. "Relax. They'll think he took a siesta. They won't figure out what happened until he starts to smell. We'll be long gone by then."

She put a hand to her mouth and gagged.

"Don't you throw up," I said. "Don't you fucking dare!"

She mumbled something.

"What? Take your hand away from your mouth."

"I want my uncle" —she swallowed— "Padré Guillermo."

It was a brief moment of weakness for her, but one that reminded me she was—despite all the posturing—still just a kid who'd wanted the security of family, someone familiar...

"I don't care if you want your fairy fucking godmother." I moved toward the door. "A little late to be getting soft, Malinal. And your uncle is probably looking for you right now—not that he'd recognise you like *that*. But if he did, he might throw you out on the streets if he found out about this little rescue mission of yours."

Her resolve returned with an angry chill that flashed through her cheeks. "So I can grow up like you?"

I raised an eyebrow at her colourful, twisted form. "I can think of worse things to be."

The smell of sour earth and burnt ozone hovers about the blood-waters of a cenote. Sometimes, if you're patient and look hard enough, you can see semi-translucent threads in the crimson, curling, twisting, like small fingers from the Otherwhere, still trying to push their way into our world.

An effect of the war, they say...

—Jorge Ortega
Aftermath

II.

The Platform's ballroom was full of VIPs, some masked, all wearing elaborate costumes for Carnival.

Scanning the crowds below from our vantage point on the mezzanine, I spotted him easily: Zorislav Durakovic. An impressive gathering followed the portly man like a devout congregation; Painted Ones of all sexes, an entourage of patterns and colours, remained two steps behind him, fanning backwards in an iridescent wave, while chupacabras perched on shoulders like gargoyles.

His bodyguards stood at strategic positions, two at each elbow, four others orbiting around like satellites.

"Remember," I whispered, "it's been five years since they took him and *changed* him. It may be difficult to spot him at first."

"He is my brother. I'll recognise him."

"You'd better, for your sake, Malinal. Timing is going to be important."

Malinal's chupacabra, mounted on her shoulders, muttered, and she reached out to stroke the creature's head. Her elongated fingers were studded with tiny, raised welts of varying colours.

Malinal had courage despite her age. She'd done what I could never do, Adalia. She became merchandise, willingly submersed herself in the blood-waters, twisting and reshaping her body into colourful alien contours; and to exist with that *thing* crawling over her, fixed to her like a virus.

She was undisciplined, and she was afraid, but she had guts, Adalia, and she trusted me. Just as you once did, trust that I'd always be there for you, trust that we'd never be parted.

You know I could never let it go, Adalia. You know it had to be done. It was why I came here…

I watched as Durakovic and his Painted Ones passed beneath us on their way to the dining hall.

"Papan…"

"What?" I whispered, turning to her.

"My brother," she said, luminous blue eyes filled with tears. *"He's not here!"*

*

I remember when they took you, Adalia, grabbed you off the streets. Someone shouted a warning. The flesh traders were coming. Adults seized what children they could and ran; others took up bricks or segments of piping to throw at the attackers.

I hid in the brush near a communal toilet block set back from the road and watched as you dashed for the safety of a crumbling shack.

You never made it.

Adults shouted insults and hurled their weapons at the passing truck. A man leaned out the passenger-side window and sprayed the street with bullets.

And in those early years, I'd never been close to finding out where they'd taken you, or if your body was even still alive.

Pulling yourself from the blood-waters, you would break through the membrane surrounding your new body. And you'd vomit out the baby creature, almost breaking your jaw. The chupacabra squeals and thrashes on the stones, muscles, and tendons showing, slick and glistening with blood.

And it lifts its arms to you, like a small child, and grips your bare legs with tiny, bloody hands and hisses and clicks its teeth.

And it will grow to become the guarantor of your obedience.

—Nadia Reyes
Interview: A Painted One Speaks

III.

I scanned the ballroom again, noting the number of armed staff, and the various exits. Escape pods clung to the outer rim of the Platform; the elevators were now underneath, secured in its belly.

I wasn't worried about getting lost, my eidetic memory wouldn't allow it. With a combination of innate skill and learned tactics, the memory of my journey through the Platform was as detailed and as vivid as you.

I pretended to watch the guests milling about the ballroom. Thinking. To escape, to quietly steal away under the Mexican moonlight below was not part of my plan. Never was.

"I suppose it was a gamble, Papan," she muttered. "There was never any real guarantee Jago would be here, despite being listed in the manifest."

She'd likely want to leave now, and I needed to stall for time.

"The data you extracted was precise," I said. "He's here." My temples throbbed, and I rubbed them with my fingers.

She cocked her head at me. "Papan. Are you okay?"

"It's a big Platform," I said. "There are other places he could be. We stick to the plan."

"You don't look well."

"I'm fine." I gripped her arm, firmly, and hurried her through the corridors, away from the ballroom and deeper into the Platform. Ahead was an access hatch, the one cutting off Durakovic's penthouse chambers from the rest of the dignitaries. Two guardsmen, dressed in black, stood on either side of the door.

I brushed my free hand across my dress and in one swift motion pulled off a metallic adornment—two thin cylinders: a double-barrelled blow dart. I raised it to my mouth and shot both guards in the neck. They struggled for only a moment as the zombie drug slammed through them, paralysing them while keeping them conscious.

Once I'd removed the darts, I rummaged through a guard's pockets and tossed Malinal a silver encryption shard. "Open the hatch." She obeyed. The door irised open, and I pushed her across the threshold.

Feeding off her tension the chupacabra grew anxious and climbed up on her back. Blood trickled down her chemise in thin red lines as its claws pricked her flesh. She bit her lip.

And then the muffled sounds of rushing water. The bathroom door opened, and a guard emerged. I pulled a long filament from the threads of my dress, cracked it like a whip, and snapped it diagonally down his body. Shock registered on the guard's face as his top half slid off and hit the floor with a wet smack.

Malinal threw up over a leather chair.

"Papan—" She dry-heaved. "*What the fuck!*"

Her chupacabra growled, and its eyes narrowed.

I tossed down the wire, reached between my legs, and pulled out the gun, silencer fixed to the barrel. I clicked off the safety.

"Papan!" Anger framed her cheeks. "You tell me what you're planning, or—" A deep snarl stopped her. She looked sideways over her shoulder. The creature had reached around, mouth near her ear, teeth glistening.

Malinal took a few deep breaths and gripped a chair for support.

I spied a door across the room. I levelled the gun over her shoulder and pushed her towards the door; her chupacabra grumbled and ducked down to her waist.

"Open it," I said.

She obeyed.

Beyond the door was a lavish bed chamber, and in the centre was a giant bed. Six Painted Ones reclined in various states of dress. Some sat up, while others remained still. All watched us with shocked expressions. Chupacabras stared from shoulder perches. I lowered my gun.

"Is he here?" I asked. "Your brother."

"No."

Strange and utterly alien eyes—eyes filled with fear—stared at me from painted faces.

It was the same fear I saw in your eyes, Adalia, as they took your living body away. I knew they'd changed you, sold you on. Sold you to Durakovic. I can only imagine what he did to you before slitting your throat and tossing your body from the top of his penthouse in Vienna.

I stared back at the painted figures on the bed. I hesitated for only a moment, then gunned them down.

Without companions, their chupacabras squealed in agony and died.

*

"You didn't have to kill them!"

"I did them a favour," I said. "Believe me."

"And what kind of favour will I get?"

"*They* didn't pay me. You did. Get your brother, and I get you both off the peninsula. That was the deal you bought."

"And what the fuck do we do now?" Her chupacabra howled with madness.

"We wait here. He'll come sooner or later. These are his rooms, after all."

"What do you mean? *He'll* come?" Her eyes lit up and she stood straight, the brassy girl from Motul once again. "You told me you wanted the prestige of breaking into a *Bastard* stronghold, but you're after Durakovic, aren't you?"

"Figure that out all by yourself, did you?"

"You used me!"

"You're welcome."

Malinal shuddered with that bitter knowledge, and her chupacabra darkened, spinal quills standing up along its arched back. It looked at her with black, penetrating eyes, and let loose an unholy growl.

"It's the flesh traders you want, Papan. They supply the demand for cartels like the *Bastards of*—"

"Durakovic created the demand!" I cried out. "He's responsible for this whole industry, started it back in Sarajevo! That's where the trail for my sister went cold. You were my chance to get close to him—"

"Sister." Malinal nodded. "You had a sister. Of course. Now it makes sense, why you spasm so often."

Pain gathered behind my eyes, and I put a hand up to my head as if to push you aside, Adalia.

"Head hurt, does it?" she said. "Papan, I *know.*"

"You know shit."

"Your sister" —she took a slow step towards me— "is in there with you, isn't she?" Malinal touched my forehead. "But somehow you haven't been overwritten; you're still here."

"Don't sound so disappointed."

"She should've displaced you."

The tears forming in my eyes angered me. I couldn't protect you, Adalia. In my guilt, I poured your backup into me, sacrificed myself to become you—the sweet, adorable, innocent girl you always were before they stole you from me. But something went wrong.

"Must've compartmentalised herself, somehow," Malinal continued, "somewhere in your head. Doesn't often happen, but it would explain your pain."

"So, I'm a rarity, but if you're thinking I'm some sort of freak show, you haven't looked in the mirror lately."

She frowned. "If you want to beat them, then live to spite them. *That* would be real justice. This is madness!"

I flung her arm away. "What do you know of justice, little girl? Or madness?"

She gripped her pendant. "Jago's living body is not here. I sacrificed my body for a chance to save him. But that doesn't mean I want to die!"

"The risk was always there."

"No! That wasn't the bargain. You made a deal, you'd get me through this, you'd get me off the peninsula. I trusted you!"

"Time to grow up, Malinal."

"*Grow up? Grow up?*" she shrieked. Her chupacabra chattered, claws flexed, kneading her already bloodied shoulders. She cried out and took a few slow breaths to calm down.

"How old was your sister when they took her?" she asked.

"Six."

"Okay. Six years old, Papan, and because she hasn't displaced you she'll remain stunted, unable to grow. In your head, she'll always be six years old, and you want to make a suicide run and take her with you. A child. Does that sound grown-up to you? Is that justice?"

I slapped her for her impertinence, and she went crashing to the floor. Her creature squealed.

"That's right, Papan," she said calmly, sitting up, "become the thing you despise most. Why don't you get yourself a hundred Painted Ones and beat the shit out of them, too!"

"Best shut your mouth, girl, or I'll shut it for you!"

"This isn't about your sister; it isn't about Durakovic. It's about a grown woman who can't deal with shit. It's about your guilt, Papan. It's about *you!*"

I shoved my gun in her face. "Last chance."

"Yes," she said, more bravely than I expected. "For all of us."

I slid my finger across the trigger.

"Papan, if you think—" Her eyes moved as she tracked beyond me to the other side of the room. I spun around.

There was a bug on the wall.

It was black, two centimetres long. A triatominae. A kissing bug. A pest carrying Chagas disease. Or at least it looked like one.

Then it spoke. "I know what you're trying to do."

A sonic explosion filled the room and tore through my cranium. My legs crumpled, the floor came up and hit my face, and a black wave of unconsciousness quickly drowned me.

The disintegration of normal political structures was total. City-states rose to fill the void, ruled by cartels. Skilled, and technologically savvy, they protect their interests with venom, view each other with deep suspicion, and often switch allegiances between themselves as quickly as you or I might change our shirts.

But none are more dangerous than the Bastards of Magdeleine, who rule Mérida with an iron fist...

—Miguel DeJesus
The Americas: A Model of Power and Survival

IV.

I awoke to voices and the rattle of a chain.

"What did you think you'd achieve, Malinal?" A deep baritone. A man's voice.

"...how can you ask me that? I came to..."

"...the *Bastards* picked up your intrusion the moment you hacked their systems. You never had a chance, girl."

I pushed myself up onto my hands. "Malinal?"

"Your friend's awake." A different voice. Tenor. Young. Male.

"Malinal?" Eyes blurred, focused. Lights burned from high chandeliers. We were in a chamber: a large domed construction of transparent plasti-glass. We were on top of the Platform.

Malinal stood at the centre of the large, empty room, looking over her shoulder at me. A figure near her, robed in black. The baritone. Next to him was the owner of the other voice, an image corrupted by the dark spectre of a chupacabra upon his shoulder.

She found her brother.

Or rather, he found her.

Jago held my gun in one hand, barrel facing the decking. In his other hand, he gripped Malinal's pendant. Naked to the waist, his skin glistened so perfectly, the bronze colouring and whirling patterns so striking, as though he stood somewhere between this world and the next.

Malinal turned back to the robed man. "Uncle Guillermo, what are you doing here? What did you do?"

"What I had to do."

As I got to my feet, I realised my jewellery was gone, my dress stripped of its accoutrements.

"They've disarmed you," the boy said without looking at me.

I snorted. "Oh, really?"

Jago ignored me and raised the gun, aimed it at the man. The swirling patterns on his face seemed to grow darker. "Uncle, answer Malinal. Go on. Tell her. You owe her that much."

It was then I noticed the metallic collar around Padré Guillermo's throat, and the chain hanging just behind his shoulder. It attached to a floor bolt next to his feet.

"And what would you have me say?" the padré said. "The war left us nothing. As a diocese, we must finance ourselves. The conflict almost bankrupted the Holy See."

"You let them take your own flesh and blood!" Jago snapped. His chupacabra hissed a warning. "Tell her about the orphanage, as well."

Outside the dome, I spied an escape pod clamped to the edge of the decking. Slowly, carefully, I peeled back the skin on my left ring finger and gripped the metallic cylinder lodged in the socket.

"So, the *Bastards* offered you a solution to your financial woes, padré," I said, "and you took it. Selling directly to them from the orphanage run by your diocese, I presume."

"Uncle!" Malinal put her hands to her mouth. "And Papa?"

"Your father never knew what I was doing." The padré looked at the barrel of the gun, at Jago. "I didn't have a choice. We needed the money."

"But you were undercutting the flesh traders, padré," I said. "That's my guess. Am I right?"

He said nothing.

"Skimming off the top of their profits," I continued. "Stupid. But you're not the first to try it."

"And from what I've heard, you're not the first bounty hunter to stand here." His face was red, as though straining with some inner truth.

Jago clicked off the gun's safety, and a guttural sound rose from the creature on his shoulder.

Malinal flinched. "Please, stop!"

"And what about Jago, padré?" I asked.

Padré Guillermo looked lost. "Classic case of wrong place, wrong time."

"Jago just happened to drop by the orphanage to see you. Correct? And why not? I mean, you are his uncle, after all."

"The *Bastards* showed up, unannounced," he said. "They demanded compensation for what I'd taken from them. They forced me to surrender a dozen children, on the spot, or they'd kill me, kill every priest in the diocese, and burn our churches to the ground. They took Jago, as well." The padré stared hard at me. "What could I do? Tell me! What could I do?"

"All I did," Jago said, "was come back from school—"

"You never answered Malinal's question, padré," I said, brusquely. "How did you come to be here?"

The padré remained silent.

"Oh, go on, *holy* man," I prodded. "Don't stop now." I leaned forward. "Confession is good for the soul."

"I asked for him to be here," Jago said. "I wanted all

of it to end. I begged them to let me end it. *Like this!*"
He pushed the gun in the padré's face. Jago's chupacabra
growled, bared its teeth, and sank its claws into his flesh.
Jago winced and gasped.

"Jago, no!" Malinal screeched; her chupacabra let loose
a sympathetic wail. "He should be punished, God knows.
But not like this. Not murder."

"Why not? Uncle killed me the day he let the *Bastards*
take me away, and I know what happened to Papa. *He* told
me." Jago gazed at Malinal desperately, voice trembling.
"This has to end."

"It can end," she said. "Leave Uncle. Come with me.
You can forget about what's happened." She motioned to
me with an arm. "Tell him, Papan, please."

"Jago, listen," I said. "I can get you both out of the city,
off the peninsula. It's all set up."

"You see, Jago," Malinal said. "We can be a family again.
With that." She pointed to the pendant.

"No, no you don't understand." Jago teetered between
anguish and despair.

And I sensed something in his voice, Adalia,
something desperate, something true…

I looked at Malinal, then Jago. I dreaded the words
before he even spoke them.

"This backup is not mine, Malinal." He held it out to
her. "It's yours."

Time stopped. Seconds of stillness. Malinal's face lit
up with horror and she doubled over, as though she'd
been pole-axed.

As she fell to her knees, I pulled the metallic implant

from my finger socket—triggering the mechanism—and threw it at the plasti-glass.

It exploded on contact.

Last year it was reported that an estimated 746 children were stolen on the Yucatan peninsula. This is a sharp increase from previous years.

—Bonita Vasquez
<u>The New Flesh</u>

V.

A klaxon sounded.

Shards of plasti-glass littered the air and clattered to the floor like coins. The chamber seemed to tilt, and the floor shifted. Air rushed through the hole like a cyclone and pulled at our clothes and hair. Below us came the muffled thud of the emergency bulkheads slamming shut. Security would have to cut their way through to reach us. For the moment, we were trapped on the roof.

I grabbed Malinal's arm and lifted her. "Let's go!"

She looked to her brother, pleadingly, but he shook his head, sorrow framing his bright yellow eyes.

"After they killed you the first time," Jago said, "they took *my* backup from your hands and destroyed it. And they took *your* backup from me. Papa entrusted me with it, remember? I had it around my neck when they tied me down..." He held the pendant up again. "Five times you've come, thinking to bring me this. And five times I've watched you die."

"Why?" she said. "I don't understand—"

His eyes, his beautiful painted eyes, leaked silver tears.

"Because you'd got it in your head you could save me. The *Bastards* thought it a fitting punishment to implant you in another each time they murdered you so that you would come back, again and again." His breath stuttered. "And you've always been so stubborn. You couldn't stay away..."

"You're just another urchin they picked up off the street, girl," said the padre, "like the other five. A body to use as they see fit."

"They're very sportive," I said, "those *Bastards of Magdeleine*."

Jago pulled back the hammer. "Well, the game ends."

"Jago," she said, "please. Don't. I'm still her. I'm still your Malinal..."

"I know." Determination set in his eyes. "With his death—so richly deserved—I'll break the cycle that brings you back. You have a chance, now. I'm doing this for your sake, and mine."

Malinal struggled against my grip and looked at me.

"He wants to die," I said; and I heard myself—*oh God, I heard myself*—unemotional, ice-cold, professional.

"Papan, please!" she wailed. "Let me go!"

"Jago, you can come with us," I said, but the boy shook his head. His chupacabra's growl became a diabolical whine, an alien noise rising to fill the air.

"Malinal," Jago said. "Leave. Take that body and live, live for me, live for Papa."

"*Jago!*" She fought me, but I pulled her close, gripped her head with both hands and turned away her face. Her chupacabra howled and wrapped its arms around her torso.

Uncle Guillermo was chanting now; the *Oratio Dominica*: "In the name of the Father, and of the Son—"

"Yes," Jago said, pushing the gun against the padré's head. "Oh, yes. In the name of the *Father*."

A shot sounded.

...sources have recently informed me that, seeing potential revenue streams in the burgeoning Eastern Eurasian slave market, the Bastards of Magdeleine have seized control of the cenote at San Ignacio.

—Bonita Vasquez
<u>The New Flesh</u>

VI.

Blood. There was so much blood. Jago's creature tore into his body. The sound of shredding flesh was loud in my ears, and crimson rivers crept slowly across the floor.

And as the beast devoured him, sliced flesh and crunched bone, Jago never made a sound.

When his chupacabra was finished, it reared up and died.

*

The pod rested in the centre of a burnt patch of long grass some fifty kilometres outside the city. I hurried Malinal through the field, her chupacabra hugging her waist, chattering.

We reached a dirt road. A few metres ahead sat the truck, ghostly in silver moonlight, bang on time. My contact was in the driver's seat, waiting.

"Here's where we part company," I said. "My man will

take you as far as Quibdó, in Colombia. You know where to go from there."

"I know. And thank you."

"You sure you're okay?"

Malinal opened her palm to reveal the pendant, her backup. She had gripped it tightly as I'd dragged her out to the pod, her gaze inward the whole time during our escape, as though looking to some other world.

There was a great deal she had to take in, Adalia, much to reckon, and she did it with courage, without tears, without fear.

With great care, Malinal closed her hand back over the pendant and held it as though it were a precious stone. Itzamná, ruler of heaven and healing.

"Am I okay?" she said softly. "I don't know. What about you?"

I turned to go.

"Papan," she called. I stopped and pivoted around.

"Back in Durakovic's chambers," she said. "Would you really have killed me?"

My voice left me, and in the silence between us, only the tall grasses spoke, whispering among themselves.

I sensed you waiting, Adalia, expectantly.

"You're alive," I said. "I've kept my end of the bargain."

Malinal stared at the pendant, stroking its carved features—features not unlike the patterns of her own twisted skin.

"Papan, please. Come with us," she said, "and live. Live for *her*."

And you spoke to me, Adalia, of the streets where we used to play, of the quiet beaches where we once collected seashells and built castles in the sand, while the blue ocean gently kissed our feet. You spoke of happier times…

"This is all I know," I said, not so much to her as to you, Adalia. "And Durakovic is still out there. How can I simply let go? How can I live any other life?"

Malinal gazed at the far horizon, then went to the truck, opened the door, and stopped and turned to face me.

"In all honesty, I don't know how you can live, Papan. I don't know how I can live, how any of us can live. But I do know one thing for certain."

"What's that?"

Malinal's eyes glistened with hope.

"There's always a choice," she said.

I smiled.

HEART OF THE CITY, HEART OF THE SEA

VOICES

It's like falling in a dream: the stomach lurches, followed by a tingling sensation that reverberates through the body with lightning speed, muscles jerk—

—and I wake, gasping as I reach the grassland on the other side of the threshold.

I wish it were a dream, and that my wife Mari would be here on the other side of the Gate of Bones, on this other plane, waiting for me.

I've always fought off the idea that she could be dead. No. Mari had simply gone off by herself. And she is either unable to return or she is unwilling.

I'm not sure which option is worse. But the guilt is mine, and it stalks me through the lonely years like a malevolent shadow.

And now I return to the land of the Tals, return to Tal-Tagier, the coral city upon the great sea, to convince her fractious twin sister, Kayla, to come home for good, to give up the shrine that she has made of Mari's room.

It'll be a struggle, but I must try.

Kayla is all the family I have left.

My companion Kovo, not quite a man yet more than a boy, holds the reins of my horse and walks beside it, the tall grass swishing about his knees. He does not talk much; however, he did seem eager to be my attendant on this journey. I welcome the company since I've few friends these days.

The grassland inclines and deposits us upon the beach. Ahead is a wide wooden bridge that spans the length of the bay to the city of raised coral, busy with Tal travellers, coming and going. The city of pastel-coloured spires and turrets glows warmly in the tropical sun and from the centre, rising into a clear cerulean sky, towering above all else, is the Temple of the City-Mother.

"Lord Banning," says Kovo, "I'm curious. Why did the duke agree to see you, and permit you to return? Is it not unusual?"

"Why? Because I'm marked?"

"You abandoned your men, walked away from the duke's council, refused to honour your duties to the Realm—"

I let the slight pass. To be truthful, I'm more amused at the boy's courage than angry at the obvious insult. He reminds me of myself at that age—blind faith, an unwavering dedication to tradition, a soul brimming with fire.

"All true," I say, hand resting on the hilt of my blade. "Regardless, the duke cannot deny me the privileges I rightfully earned as his champion and then emissary to these people. And besides" —I lean down from the saddle— "maybe the old goat still likes me."

Kovo's attempt at a smile resembles the sneer on a stone gargoyle.

A tropical breeze comes in off the sea in a steady cadence, bringing with it an uncanny murmuring.

Kovo tenses; his hand grips the blade at his side.

I laugh. "Easy, young Kovo, and who do you intend to cut?"

"What is that?"

"The Tals believe the city sings with the many voices of the dead. Know what I think? It's the wind, piping through the many honeycombed passages in the coral." I pat his shoulder. "Still, it makes the hair bristle on the back of the neck, doesn't it?"

"Your horse. He's not spooked."

"He never is. Maybe he's made of stronger stuff."

Kovo's face is granite. "I've served many lords, and travelled widely. I fear nothing and no one."

I shrug. "As you say."

Kovo considers our surroundings. "Is this land cursed?"

"Does it matter?"

He glances at the city, utters a prayer.

"Save your supplications, young Kovo," I say. "The god of our realm does not hear you in this place."

"If you don't mind, Lord Banning," says Kovo, brusquely, "I prefer to stay true to the customs of our people."

"Of course, but be mindful, you have much to learn."

There's the steady clomping of my horse's hooves across wooden boards. We're crossing the bridge. The murmuring voices now surround us. Despite his protestations, I still think Kovo looks anxious and uncertain.

"Keep your hand away from your blade," I say. "The Tals will generally ignore us, but if they feel threatened, well, I've come for Kayla. It's not my intention to start a fight."

"Then it's true what they say—that you no longer have the stomach for it."

I keep my gaze ahead. "I like you, young Kovo, but don't press your luck. You take a lot of chances with that mouth."

IN THE CITY PROPER

We're stopped at the gates, where I take a folded piece of parchment from my belt and hand it to the guard. The Tal man cannot read the written language of my people, so he spies the duke's seal at the bottom of the paper and studies it. Seeming convinced it's not a forgery he hands the letter back and steps aside.

Beyond the city gate is a coral outcropping complete with a livery. I stable the horse, for no animal may go any further, and we walk the short concourse to a wood and chain walkway, where the rippling waters of a canal run underneath. We reach the other side and pass into the city proper. Here, laughter echoes from high windows and children screech through alleyways, seeming to appear from nowhere, only to disappear with equal skill.

And here, Tal men and women walk with purpose; some chant while others stop to whisper their secret thoughts into the pores of the coral prayer columns that sprout up and down the thoroughfare. Between coral spires shallow canals run their courses, and boats pass quietly in the slow-moving water.

A group of children emerge from a tunnel at street level, one of many open rain gutters, and sprint across our path. A girl with emerald eyes runs into me, silver bells braided into her auburn hair.

I grip the child by the arms to stop her from falling.

"Sorry, little one," I say.

She catches her breath and smiles up at me.

"Are you hurt?" I ask.

She shakes her head; the bells chime sweetly.

A deep-throated growl rumbles out of the shadows ahead of me. "*You!*"

The old witch stands in the shadowed mouth of an alley, staff in hand. The girl and her companions rush past the wrinkled crone and disappear into the gloom behind her.

"I know that voice," I say. Kovo is about to speak but I stop him with a cold glance. "Say nothing; do nothing."

Kovo bows.

The woman steps into the sunlight. Her face is a gnarled piece of bark, and her once-youthful skin is stained parchment.

"Greetings, Muan." I step forward. "It's been a long time, but I see the City-Mother still favours you."

"Don't give me your platitudes, Lord Banning," she hisses. "Don't you dare!"

"I speak the truth, Muan."

"You never spoke a true word in your life, and you know it." She points a bony finger at me. "Never spoke a true word to your wife, Mari, did you?"

I bristle. "What do you know of it, witch?"

"More than you'd care to admit," she says.

"I did what you demanded of me, Muan. I stayed away."

"And now you're back. Don't bother showing me the letter, I knew you'd come."

"Then you know why I'm here."

"I do, but what makes you think you can convince Kayla to return? You couldn't even keep your wife!" She wrinkles her lips. "It matters not. You're too late. Kayla belongs to us now."

Cold fingers dance up my back. "You lie."

"It pleases me to disappoint you. Don't believe me? Ask her yourself. You know where to find her."

"Kayla comes here once a month to visit her sister's room and mourn, not to give herself as a sacrifice to your City-Mother. No doubt this is *your* doing."

Muan waves away my words. "She took the Temple vow, at the darkening of the moon, three nights ago. Soon she'll be where you can no longer hurt her like you did your wife, year after year. Sorry, Lord Banning, as I couldn't help you before, so I can't help you now."

"Listen, old woman—"

"Don't 'old woman' me! You're not so young yourself. Kayla tells me you're marked. Given up everything, eh? How very big of you, mighty warrior. So, your job now is the woeful husband? It doesn't suit you."

"You mock my pain?"

"No," she says. "I mock you!"

Kovo gasps and calls out, "My Lord—"

I raise a hand to silence him.

Muan screws up one eye, and studies Kovo as though reading a text. "Best watch that dog of yours. I'm not convinced he's tame."

A single, deep note rings out from every pore of the

city; the air vibrates against my skin. It's the Temple call to prayer. The old woman turns to go.

"Muan, wait!"

"Go to Kayla, speak with her," Muan says. "And when she's done with you, leave and never return. I've always despised you, Emissary of the Duke from the Land Beyond the Bones. Don't give me a reason to show you how much."

I stare after her, eyes watery in my head. Shuffling nearby has me look down at two emerald eyes that stare out at me from an open rain gutter.

Kovo walks forward, hand on his hip. I backhand him for his disobedience.

WORDS THAT STRIKE LIKE LIGHTNING

Mari's room, our old residence, is situated at the top of a grand coral tower. Below, a canal runs between the street and the inn. I climb the few steps to the flyover, turn and place my hand on Kovo's shoulder.

"Remain here," I say. "What I have to say to my wife's sister is none of your concern."

"And how that witch spoke to you?" he says. "Is that none of *your* concern?"

I poke my finger in his chest. "Do as I say."

He stays put, eyes blazing with a cold light.

The walkway sways slightly with my steps. I reach the portico, speak with the proprietor, and ascend the stairs to the top landing. When I try the door it is unlocked, and pushing it wide I look into the room.

It's all there, as I knew it would be—Mari's easel, leather-bound sketchbooks, coloured chalk, ceramic pots of paint; even the paintings she'd laboured over still lean, unframed, against chairs and tables. It's as though she's just been here, and only recently left to search the streets for inspiration.

And sitting on a stool with her back to me is Kayla. Her black hair is unkempt, and her grey tunic clings to her skin. She sits before a self-portrait of her sister. In the painting, Mari's hair is tied up on her head, arms resting in her lap. Around Mari's wrist is the brass and copper knotted cuff bracelet I gave her after we buried our son.

"Kayla."

She turns. Her face is thin, and her eyes are sunken. She wears the pale, ashen look of the dead. Kayla stares for a moment, then turns back to her sister's portrait.

"Mari has my face," Kayla says, "but she's nothing like me. You knew that. She was the best of both of us: soft-spoken, delicate. And you shattered her like porcelain."

"This conversation has long since worn out. I've come to bring you home."

"You mean you've come to save the troubled sister, to ease your guilty conscience. A wife who abandoned you and a dead sister-in-law too much for you to handle?"

I spring forward, grab Kayla's shoulders, pull her to her feet and spin her around. "Is what Muan told me true? About you taking the vow?"

"And if it is?"

"This is not what Mari would've wanted for you."

She utters a small cry of contempt. "Suddenly, you care what my sister wants. Why now?"

It's a good question. I have no answer.

"You couldn't handle me, so you married *her*," Kayla

spits. "Why? Was it out of spite? Do you hate me so much?"

I let her go. "You have it wrong. And you flatter yourself."

"Do I?"

"We all make our choices."

"Your choices were always the same," she says. "Blind faith in your duties, your obligations to the duke."

Her words strike like lightning. All my life I've been faithful to another man and his ideals, acting with stone confidence, believing I was part of something bigger than myself, something virtuous and just.

Duties. Obligations. Words I once believed in. Words that now ring hollow in an old man's chest.

"I did what I had to do, Kayla."

"For the duke and his bloody wars," she says, "but never for my sister."

I struggle to keep my chin up. "She knew what her life would be."

"Her life was unavoidable the minute you chose her! Who could refuse the duke's champion?"

"That's enough, Kayla."

"Where were you all those days and nights? She was sick with worry, sick not knowing if you were alive. Where were you when she needed comfort as your son came stillborn into the world? Out on the battlefield, that's where!"

"And where were you? Off in the mountain villages to soothe your jealousy."

"I left because I hated what you'd done to her, how you came and went as you pleased, condemning her to a life of uncertainty. And when you could no longer fight the duke's battles you became emissary and dragged her to this place."

"Enough!"

"Do you feel nothing at all? Did you ever? Mari was your wife—"

"Kayla, I warn you—"

"—and my sister."

"And she insisted I bring her here!" I'd never said it before. Never out loud, anyway. And now it's there, lingering in the air between us.

Kayla's eyes widen.

"You dare lay this at her feet!" She reaches to the nearest table where she grabs a fistful of paint brushes and hurls them. I bring my hands to my face; the brushes pelt my arms and scatter about the room.

"She came because she didn't deserve to be alone!" She snatches up a ceramic pot of paint and throws it. It soars past my ear and shatters on the coral wall behind me. "Again, and again, always alone!"

I try to utter something, but the words remain a jumble in my throat.

"She came because she needed you to love her, to spare her a few scraps of your precious time." She flings a sketchbook so that it flutters over my head, falls to the floor, and dies.

"Kayla, listen—"

"It's done, Banning," she says. "Muan offered me peace, *real* peace, and by the Nine Hells, peace I will have."

"How? By sacrificing yourself on some foreign altar—"

She stumbles to the door, opens it, and stops.

"Mari deserved better than you, Banning. Much better." Kayla leans against the doorframe and squeezes her eyes shut. "And a better sister than me."

She slams the door.

VERMILION LIGHT

I purchased a room for Kovo at an inn down the city's main street and returned to the room that was once my home, Mari's home, for several months.

I was the first and only emissary allowed in this land. No outsider had ever set foot in the great city on the sea. Trade is restricted to the area around the Gate of Bones, and we've always honoured that agreement, for their medicines are powerful and necessary for the duke's armies. We cannot replicate their remedies, and the Tal witches would rather die than give us the secret, so the agreement suits our needs.

It's now three in the morning by the Tal clock, and Kayla has not returned. I'm not overly surprised.

I light an oil lamp, lie on the bed, and stare at the darkened ceiling. Anger sits in my heart—anger at Kayla's stubbornness, at her waspish tongue that stabbed me with truth.

If only I gave Mari the home she wanted, the home she deserved, a home filled with our love. But I was young and full of ambition, a warrior driven to kill the duke's enemies.

And I trusted that, later, when I became old, tired, and the anger had burned out, I'd leave her no more. Later, I'd rejoice in her laughter and her company; later, she'd have all she desired.

Later, I promised her. Always later.

Until it was too late.

Outside, the wind came off the great sea, and from the city's many towers and minarets, a gentle singing begins, hanging thinly on the air like a ghostly choir.

*

Kayla returns at some point before dawn. She doesn't question why I'm still here, but stomps forward to the bed and throws herself down next to me. I say nothing until she surprises me with a question she'd never asked in the years since Mari disappeared. "Do you think she knew what happened between us that night?"

I get up and go to the window, push aside the curtains, and lean out over the sill. Below, the streets and canals murmur with the hushed conversations and low laughter of night people. The moon has long since dropped behind the sea, and in the sky the stars shine like crystals set into a black stone.

"I don't know," I say, though I remember the night in question. It was eighteen years ago; the war with the Estuary Chieftains was over, and I returned to the capitol. That same night Kayla came back from her self-imposed exile in the mountain villages. The celebrations went on through the month of harvest, thirty days of madness.

"I should've stayed away," she says.

"I had too much wine that night, Kayla. We both did."

"I took advantage of your drunkenness."

I want to say: No, you didn't. Even full of drink I knew the difference between them, the different ways they touched me, the different ways they kissed. Kayla's mouth tried to devour me, her passion a coil let loose, releasing its energy in a mad frenzy. Mari was slow, deliberate, building up to a steady fire.

And drunkenness, its own form of madness, allowed me to take what I wanted then, without thought or reason.

"You were right," she says. "Jealousy made me run away."

"And you were wrong. I didn't marry your sister out of spite. Both our lives, Kayla, were filled with uncertainty and chaos. It was the stillness of her soul that enchanted me, a stillness I wanted and hoped—one day—would cleanse the years of blood from my hands."

Kayla's breathing is stuttered, and I know she's crying.

"And when my reflexes slowed, I came here as an emissary," I continue. "One last duty to perform for my duke."

"Never did know how to quit, did you?" A small laugh. "Neither did I."

"Whether you like it or not, I'm all you have left. We are kin. Renounce your vow, Kayla, and come home."

"To live with you? To share laughter and the warmth of a home?" She considers her stomach and rubs it slowly with both hands.

Off in the distance, the Temple calls out its single, deep note that vibrates through the city, calling to the faithful.

"No," I say, "but to live your life."

Whatever she utters next is drowned in a storm of tears.

I remain at the window until the dawn fills the room with a cool vermilion light.

*

Kayla cries herself to sleep.

In the warmth of the advancing morning, and with the murmuring voices from the coral minarets in my ears, I sit in a chair and finally sleep.

When I wake, Kayla is gone.

DANGEROUS CONFIDENCE

I don't go looking for her but wander, aimlessly, like a man struck blind. I buy food from street vendors and sleep in a dark corner of an all-night tavern, tankard in hand.

I can't go back to the room. I can't face the woman with my wife's face. For what can I say now to change her mind? What could I ever have said?

I look into my near-empty tankard. I consider drinking the remains; instead, I push the mug away and leave. In the haze of my drunkenness, I lose track of the hours, and it is night once again.

Lanterns perched high upon metal posts cast pools of soft yellow light, barely bright enough to penetrate the gloom. Occasionally, a man or woman passes me, quick and silent, trading glances with me before disappearing into the black maw of an alley.

I'm at a dockyard, where small Tal boats rock gently in their berths, and the slow rolling of the sea brings a comforting stillness to my heart. And as a night breeze blows up and the city begins to sing, I sit on an overturned crate and listen to the soft fluted voices rise and fall in my ears.

The dullness from drink is abating and my mind clears, so much so that I can discern, just over my shoulder, the hiss of a blade being drawn from its leather sheath.

My throat croaks the name, "Kovo." I sense his hesitation, jump up, turn, and slap the weapon from his hand. "To be taken off guard so easily with a simple utterance. That was your first mistake."

Kovo's face darkens.

I've always known someone would eventually come for me, and the thought of my would-be killer being Kovo did at one point cross my mind when I first took him on. But I buried those suspicions, for I liked this young man. And that was *my* mistake.

"A mere *boy*-assassin," I mock him. "So, the Guild's sending children now. Their standards must be slipping."

Kovo swings his fist, but I catch it in mid-air, and twist the wrist hard, almost breaking bones. He goes down on one knee but doesn't scream.

"Tell me, do I seem so old and drunk to you now?" I lean in, so close I can feel the boy's breath upon my cheeks. "Who hired you? Was it that black-hearted swine, Lord Cingris?"

Kovo says between teeth, "You walked away from your honoured duties, walked away from your men, from your duke. You turned your back on everything we are!"

"And what are we?" I don't give him a chance to answer. "I've sacrificed my life, spilt enough blood, and when the time came to show something for it there was nothing there. A gaping hole of nothingness" —I bang a fist on my chest— "right here!"

"You wear the clothes of a warrior," Kovo says, "but you talk like a traitor."

I sense in him a dangerous confidence. "And what will you get in return for my death? A place of honour among fools; the praise of an idle man enthroned in a high palace?"

With a flash of silver, a searing white heat tears through my shoulder. A throwing spike. Kovo pulled it from his boot with his free hand, and the spike now bites deep into my flesh, Kovo's palm against the flat end, pushing hard.

I kick him away, and he tumbles across the dock. After removing the spike, I toss it aside and put a hand down on a crate to steady myself, breathing heavily through the pain. Now it is I who have been caught off guard, getting too close to an armed assailant.

"You're soft," says Kovo. "Your judgement clouded."

"Perhaps, but remember I said you had a lot to learn; part of that is knowing when to walk away. I'm giving you that chance."

Kovo digs into his shirt pocket, pulls out a coin, and tosses it to me. It clatters at my feet. "Have another drink, old man."

My disappointment stings. "I see."

Kovo shoots to his feet and moves his hand, quick and sharp. My instincts are still there, and I throw myself down and roll away as another spike slams into the side of the crate where I just stood. I push myself up, slowly, betrayed by my wounded shoulder.

The crack of leather comes as I lurch to my feet. Something cuts through my linen shirt and tears at the skin of my back, gouging out the meat in hot strips. I whirl around. Kovo had removed his braided leather belt and held it like a whip, the loose strands at the end knotted with small pieces of metal. Kovo's belt has become a scourge.

He flicks his belt again but this time I catch the loose strands, wrap them around my hand—despite some of the metal shards slicing deep into my palm—and pull. Kovo stumbles forward, and I grip him by the throat and squeeze. His larynx crunches beneath my fingers.

Kovo claws at my fist, sputtering for air, eyes alive with agony. I spin him around, wrap an arm across his shoulders, the other around his head, and yank. A clean, crisp snap.

Kovo stops struggling.

"Look what you made me do," I whisper, holding his corpse in my arms. "I was done with killing. It was all behind me, and you brought it back." I set his body down, gently. "You could've had a wife of your own, and maybe a son to cherish. You could've had a home and laughter."

I lean over Kovo's body for a long time, until tears burst from my eyes, and my mouth lets loose an anguished wail.

NOT COMING BACK

Dawn cracks the eastern horizon, and Tal men begin spilling on to the dock to prepare their boats for the morning's fishing. The sea is still calm, and the singing voices are now silent.

With some difficulty, I drag Kovo's body to one of the fishermen. The Tal man, expressionless, looks at the corpse, and then at me.

"Would you please, good sir," I say, "bury him at sea."

At first, the man refuses. I take off my silver bracelet,

inscribed with the duke's name, and hand it over. The Tal man hesitates, then without a word snatches the bracelet from my hand, and I help him put Kovo's body into a boat. I make the Tal gesture of thanks, but the man turns his back to me and carries on with his work.

It's been a long time since I've prayed to our god, but I pray over Kovo now. He would want that—

My wounds need proper tending, but no apothecary will treat me. Though the Tals honoured the duke's request for me to enter the city I no longer possess my special status. They owe me nothing.

I go down to the water and remove my bloodied shirt. Cupping my hands, I scoop up the water, wash out my shoulder wound, and splash some onto the deep cuts on my back. The brine stings. I tear off part of a sleeve, bunch it up, and press it against the still-bleeding gash in my shoulder.

I will speak with Kayla one last time, though it will do no good, but I must be convinced in my heart that I've done my best, for Mari's sake. When I return to the inn, Kayla is no longer there.

"She's gone," says the proprietor, clearly troubled by the bloodied cloth I hold to my naked shoulder. "When the sun rose, she was summoned to the City-Mother. She's not coming back."

Gone. To the Temple.

Muan's voice echoes in my head: *But what makes you think you can convince Kayla to return? You couldn't even keep your wife!*

Truth is hard and unyielding.

Hall of Audiences

All my life I've been certain of my reward. My obedience and my duties were my guarantors. I lived my life by it.

Wisdom comes with age, it's said. I look at my empty hands, old, scarred, worn, unable to change a thing, and only now do I fully understand the irony in that remark.

I curse the man I've become and hate the man I once was all the more.

The proprietor offers me some boiled tree-sap from his medicine cupboard, which I smear over my shoulder wound. A temporary seal. He's always been good to me. Maybe it's because I've paid him large sums over the years for the room at the top of the stairs. My back wounds still sting but have begun to crust over.

The streets of the city are busy, Tals coming and going in the glow of the morning light; some eat and drink on warm patios, while others whisper into the holes in the coral columns. In the canals between spires, slim boats pass by. Life goes on.

And so must I. To my fate.

A barren home.

I turn a corner and feel a small hand on my arm. I stop and look down. A young girl stands there, emerald-eyed and smiling.

"Hello again, little one." The girl's playmates are nowhere to be seen. "But where are your friends?"

She tugs at my arm.

"You wish me to come with you. Is that it?" I shake my head. "I leave today."

An urgency fills her eyes, and only then do I notice one fist is balled-up tightly.

The child lets go of me, and I get down on my haunches. She takes a few steps back into a lane drenched in morning shadow and holds out the fist. She spreads open her fingers.

And there, in her palm, is Mari's bracelet.

My heart pounds. "Where did you get this?"

She scurries off into the shadows and, filled with confusion and a strange sort of hope, I go after her. I cannot see the child, but I hear her, scurrying around. I follow the noise for some time, calling to her, until the lanes are so narrow they are little more than thin spaces between high coral walls.

I turn a corner and the noise stops. I'm about to call out when I hear movement from a passage at my feet. I bend down and look inside. The girl is there, a small shadow at the mouth of darkness. She's crawling backwards now, moving deeper into the tunnel. I crawl in after her. I still can't see the child, but I hear her scuffling ahead of me. I crawl some distance, but I fear I'm losing her. My wounded shoulder is slowing me.

And then silence again.

I whirl my head about in the darkness, reach out a hand, and feel other tunnels branching off. Which direction? I'm trembling in an angry panic.

"Child! *Child!*"

A faint light gleams down one of the tunnels that flickers every so often. Torchlight. I move towards it, and the tunnel opens into a large cavity. Down here coral and stone meet: a stone pedestal upon which the great city above rests. If there's a ceiling, it's far above me in the shadows. I must be in the Temple. More precisely, under it. It's no more than a tall, hollow tube of coral. A pungent smell of brine fills the room, and something else...

A soft splash echoes in my ears. Not far ahead, where the torchlight fades, I make out the sandy edge of a large pool of water. A form moves across its surface, long, slick and black.

I take a torch from its wall-mount and proceed until I'm ankle-deep in the water. A multitude of greasy black tendrils glides across the surface of the water in a slithering dance, and I think it is a nest of eels. I quickly realise my mistake. Holding the torch higher I catch a glimpse of something looming over me, stretching up into the darkness of the hollow coral. Muscles tense I take a step back, hand on the hilt of my blade.

"So, you've come," someone says over my shoulder. I whip my head around. It's Muan; her voice rebounds insidiously throughout the chamber. "This is the Hall of Audiences, where no Outsider has any right to be."

As if Muan can read my mind, she says, "The child and your wife's trinket: they were merely a way of getting you here, unseen."

"To what end?"

Muan grunts and points toward the pool. "Ask her."

I hold the torch out in front of me and, in its glow, I can just discern a figure kneeling in the water. Kayla. A black tendril is wrapped around her waist. As I step forward, the light from the torch reveals other forms in the water, great lumps wrapped by tendrils, half-submerged in the water. Four of them, at least. A wrapped tendril moves, and from between the coils a Tal face peeks out at me, grey and lifeless.

Revulsion pools in my gut.

Just then Kayla turns to me, as if from a reverie, eyes filled with a strange glow. Great tears are running down her cheeks. "I'm glad you've come."

With my free hand, I pull on the tendril about her waist but it's stronger than it appears. I reach for my blade.

Kayla puts her hand on my arm. "No."

"Please don't do it, Kayla," I say, then shout to Muan, "Why am I here, witch? Is this some cruel punishment? To make me watch as she becomes fodder for your beast?"

Muan leans forward on her staff. "No, Lord Banning. You're here to be given a chance. And it was not I who summoned you."

Pinpricks around my thigh draw my gaze. A tendril has wrapped itself up my leg. Panic, and the creature's poison, course through my veins.

The world lurches, and I'm dislocated from myself. The chamber wavers, as if under a timeless water and everything's sharp and clear—every crevice, every hole in the coral is known to me. There are no shadows, no darkness, everything glows with its own light. And the sea! I sense its rhythms, feel it pulsing and alive.

And the beast, their goddess, their City-Mother, shimmers with a bright luminescence, growing in strength, until she is a towering column of blue-white light.

Something touches my mind—something familiar.

"We have been given this moment, Lord Banning." A

gentle voice, delicate yet full of warmth. "Put your fear aside."

"No." I shake my head, denying her words, refusing her soft voice. "You're not here; you're not *her*; you're not Mari."

"I am here, my husband, as is the one who allowed me to summon you." I sense something else with us, vast and as furtive as the night sky—the eternal mind of their goddess, the City-Mother. "We are both here."

The column of blue-white light moves like folds of skin being pulled apart; an image forms and is expelled like a new-born into the world.

Mari is there, standing before the light that is the Tal goddess, feet barely touching the water. Her beauty is so clear, so radiant, it's almost painful to the eyes.

I call out to Kayla, but she's covered her face with her hands. I turn to the image of my wife. "Mari..."

She puts out a hand and a shock rips through me, a burning sensation, and a terrible knowledge is imparted to me, of the small boat Mari cast off in late at night, of the poison she'd drunk, of the fishermen who found her at dawn, barely alive, and brought her back to Tal-Tagier, back to the witch, Muan.

"Old woman," —my voice shakes— "what have you done?"

"Offered her another way," says Muan. "Death is your way, Lord Banning, not ours. Only here could she find another peace, one she could never have had in death or with *you!*"

I tremble. "All this time you held my answer, and you never saw fit to tell me."

"I told you what you deserved to know," Muan snaps. *"Nothing!"*

I look at the image of my wife through stinging tears. "On my soul, Mari, I never suspected, never allowed myself to believe that I could injure you so much."

"The past cannot be changed," she says, "but it can be reckoned with."

I try to swallow a howl of despair, but it seeps from my throat, nonetheless. "I didn't love you enough, not as I should've. I know this."

"You searched for me, did you not?" She smiles. "In that, your love was enough."

"I failed you," I insist. "Why summon me now?"

"Because it is time to put an end to all of this," she says. "For both of you."

Another shock strikes me, and burns one word into my mind: *child.*

Child? Our son had died, and Mari could have no other—

And then I remember the festival, the madness of those nights. I remember Kayla leaving again for the mountains not long after...

The space before me shimmers, and I see a field of spring flowers. A small girl, maybe four years old, walks among the coloured blossoms, her hair black and flowing beyond her shoulders. She looks every bit like her mother.

My mind reels. "A daughter?"

"Please don't send me away," Kayla whispers. "You were always the wise one. My better side—"

"Dear sister," Mari says, "now is not the time."

Tears run freely down my face. "Mari, I did not know. Kayla never told me."

"I knew my sister loved you," Mari says, "that she was bitter at our marriage, though she tried to hide it. And when Kayla discovered she was carrying your child, it was I who sent her away, swearing us both to secrecy. That was my shame, but I was angry. Angry at myself for not confronting you enough when I was your wife, angry at my barren womb. Angry with both of you."

"And if I'd told you, Lord Banning," Kayla says, "would it have made any difference?"

I wonder what it would've been like to hold the child in my arms, to hear her small, joyous laugh, to watch her sleep. But that was eighteen years ago, and many wars were still to be fought, many victories claimed.

I think of Mari. Would things have changed for us if our son had been born alive? Did I have it in me to make the sacrifices required to be a father and a husband?

I hang my head, ashamed of my answer. "No, Kayla, I wouldn't have changed for you any more than I would have for Mari. I was never much of a husband, and I could never have been a father. Not then" —I look at my old and guilty hands— "and not now."

Mari turns to Kayla. "In many matters, you always sought my advice, dear sister, but seldom took it. I implore you to heed my advice now: do not leave your daughter alone in the world. Go to her. Though she is now of age, she is still in need of a mother's love."

"It's been difficult without you—"

"She needs you, Kayla. Your memories are strong and tell me much about her. And with such knowledge I cannot, in good conscience, take you from her now. I would not ask it of you dear sister if I did not think you had the strength. One day, when the time is right, you will be allowed to return to Tal-Tagier. And when you do, call my name, speak your love for me into the coral, and the City-Mother will summon you, and we will be together, two halves made one, as we were always meant to be."

Kayla sobs quietly.

"Promise me this, my sister. That you will return to her."

Kayla breathes deeply, and her expression is that of quiet acceptance. "I promise."

Muan moves to help Kayla to her feet as the tendril slips from her waist and retreats into the water. "I will see that you get back safely," the old witch says.

Mari's attention returns to me. "Lord Banning, you are tired, and the long years have been so very dark, so very cold."

"I don't expect forgiveness," I say.

"Forgiveness is the gift I freely offer you," she says, "the gift of peace, a peace beyond mere death. Come, Lord Banning, once my husband, it is time to wash the years of blood and guilt from your hands."

Something warm touches me, as though a hand were caressing my face, and all my fear, all my revulsion at first seeing the Tal goddess, is strangely swept away. There is no anger, no shame, no guilt, only love.

"Muan," I offer the witch a smile. "I thought you said you couldn't help me."

The old witch holds Kayla's arm. "Believe me, Lord

Banning, it was not my decision. But the City-Mother is not without compassion."

"Even if it is misplaced."

Muan purses her ancient lips. "As you say."

"Kayla," I call out. "I'm sorry. For everything."

"As am I."

"And tell our daughter the truth. All of it."

Kayla nods.

Mari's image fades now, until only the pillar of light that is the City-Mother, the goddess of the Tals, stands before me.

"Come, Lord Banning…" Mari's voice echoes in my ears, sweet, and soft. "…once my husband. It is time."

I walk deeper into the water, deeper into the tendrils of my salvation, the years of blood and loneliness ebbing like a retreating tide. And as the light swallows me, I give thanks to the Tal goddess and the love that lives within her, a love that reaches out to me from the city's vast, beating heart…

SLIPPING SIDEWAYS

We buried Rachel in the spring. Not long after, Leo became a recluse. In all honesty, I never thought I'd see him again.

He stood now between the open balcony doors of his penthouse flat, perfectly framed against Geneva's dusky skyline. His hairline had receded somewhat, and he was noticeably greyer at the temples. His clothes—well, Leo had never been into fashion: tan trousers, checked shirt with a dark navy sweater draped over his shoulders—the uniform of the self-absorbed academic (on leave from a team working with the Large Hadron Collider, I'd been told).

But what really unsettled me was his expression. The mask of painful remorse had been replaced by a wild and penetrating stare. It was as though he looked at you and through you.

"Sorry I haven't called, Džemo," he said.

"It's only been six months." I twirled my whiskey glass between my fingers. "But it's understandable."

"I'm glad you're so...forgiving," he replied.

The hair on my arms stood up. I've always been a bit suspicious, maybe even slightly paranoid. I mean when you've been sleeping with your friend's wife it's kind of, well, obvious. Isn't it? Something changes in the atmosphere of a room when you enter it, and she turns to stare at you. There's something in the way her eyes play across the features of your face, her body shifting from one foot to the other, as though she were expecting you to rush into her arms.

"To forgive is divine," I said, forcing a smile.

"So they say." He said no more for several minutes. "There's a reason I finally called you."

Here it comes. My chest tightened. I hated being confronted by the truth. Once exposed, I'd have to acknowledge its existence. It was much easier to put it to the side, ignore it, and enjoy the fantasies I'd created for myself. Growing up in Sarajevo during the war, such escapism was a mode of survival. Over the years, I'd turned my made-up worlds into stories, lies spun out across hundreds of pages. I created characters I wished I could've been, and they lived lives I wished were mine.

Falling in love. With Rachel.

What finally destroyed her, and drove her to suicide, was being stuck between a reality she found untenable, and a fantasy that could never be real.

I had no doubt she loved Leo; I heard it in the way she spoke of him. But it was a love burned to cinders by neglect.

A thin, bookish man, Leo was habitually reserved, uninspired, and useless at parties. And it was this remoteness, coupled with his dull appearance and social inadequacies, which eventually drove Rachel into my arms.

"Did you know your peripheral vision is very sensitive to motion?" He turned and retreated slowly into the room.

Confusion quickly replaced my anticipation of a verbal lashing. "Is that so?"

"It is," he said. "We've all seen things out of the corners of our eyes—objects moving swiftly, vague images hurrying by as we turn a corner, things that register as unfamiliar and startle us but, when we turn, there's nothing there."

"Okay, Leo."

"These things we see are mostly smudged, blurred, but occasionally they take form, if only for the briefest of seconds. It's as though our world seemed to wink, and in doing so exposed to us something previously unseen."

"I once thought I saw a furry creature jump out at me. But, of course, I was drunk at the time."

He frowned at my lame attempt at humour.

"Come on, Leo. Where are you going with this, anyway? This seems a bit metaphysical for a scientific guy like you."

"What is metaphysics," he said, "but an attempt to understand the fundamental perceptions by which others see the world? Existence, space, time, and causality are all concepts that go well beyond mere ontology, which simply seeks to categorise things within some artificially conceived hierarchy—nonsense groupings by which we can make sense of things we can never fully explain."

"Come off it, Leo! Have you suddenly taken to reading *The Fortean Times* or something?"

"In many ways, Džemo, metaphysics may be a better word to use than science." He hurried back to the balcony to face the city and the stars like a man possessed. "The

Greek word 'metá' simply means beyond. Metaphysics. Well, what is *beyond* physics? Do you know?"

"No, I don't."

"Well, I do," he said.

Not only did he appear like a man on the edge, but he was beginning to talk like one, too. I took in the clutter of books and periodicals scattered across the room. Mirrors on opposite walls duplicated the chaos, spreading it outwards until the vision became insubstantial.

And in the middle of all this, on a small table by the sofa, stood a single picture of Rachel.

"Leo." I suddenly felt braver than I probably looked. "You can't shut yourself away from the world like this. It's been six months. I know it's hard, but you need to find a way to move on."

"I have moved on," he said. "That's why I called you here. To let you know."

I was stunned. "That's great, Leo."

He shook his head but kept his back to me, his face to the city and the sky. "No, Džemo. My perceptions have moved on; those are the first things one notices."

"You've lost me. If I'm honest, you lost me a while ago."

"I've *seen* her," he said. "Several times. Out of the corner of my eye. Passing in the streets. Going by in a taxi. It's Rachel, Džemo, and she's out there."

I went cold. *He's delirious. Or losing his mind.*

"You remember, Džemo, the controversy when they began testing the Large Hadron Collider at higher outputs for the first time? Everyone thought it would create a black hole that would swallow the earth." He laughed.

"What the hell are you talking about?"

"The collider," he said, "not only proved superstring theory but takes it in a whole new direction. Don't you see? It's created weak points in our universe, points where we can see into another reality, another *universe*. Physical movement across the planes must be possible. Somehow—"

"Leo, you need help. A counsellor, perhaps…"

He turned on me. "You of all people should appreciate possibilities and speculations. Now imagine the collider has not only fulfilled its potential but gone beyond anyone's wildest expectations. Do you understand?"

I stared into my empty glass.

"An electron can occupy numerous states simultaneously," he said. "Quantum mechanics allows this, and successful experiments in demonstrating superpositions in larger objects are old hat." He paused and seemed desperate for words. "Beryllium ion, for instance. By laser-cooling it to zero-point energy, a series of laser pulses sets it in different states, each spatially separate and coherent. Two possible states for one object!"

"Leo—"

"It's Schrödinger's cat. It's both alive and dead. I observe only one possible outcome because when I detect the object, I am entangled with it. That is, because I have seen one version of the cat, I now have a relationship with it, of a sort. Quantum decoherence prevents me from experiencing another possibility, another universe." He stepped toward me. "The collider solved this problem, in a way. We can see other possibilities, but only peripherally, like a geometrical tangent. It touches a curve and for a moment, they travel in the same direction."

"I think I'd better leave."

"There are worlds out there," he said, "side-by-side with ours. Worlds where you and I and Rachel never met. Worlds where Rachel never died. Do you know what this means? For me? And you?"

My hands were shaking as I put down the glass. Tears blurred my vision. For the first time in my life, truth, somehow, managed to win out over lies.

"I loved her, too," I said.

"I know." His tone was surprisingly gentle. "It's a second chance. For both of us."

I wouldn't listen anymore. Fantasies were my job. But the one reality, the one hard concrete fact I could never bury underneath all my words was the fact that Rachel was gone.

His Rachel. My Rachel. And no amount of grief-fuelled, half-cocked, drunken school-boy speculation was going to bring her back.

And I shared my portion of the blame for that.

"Good-bye, Leo." I moved for the door.

"I don't blame you," he called after me. "Just wanted you to know that."

I left.

*

I screwed up my courage and returned to his flat a few days later, but he didn't answer the buzzer. When the police entered, they found no trace of him. They never found his body. Anywhere.

Some nights, when the sky was particularly clear, and the moon had risen, full and bold, I imagined I'd seen him out of the corner of my eye, walking around the bend of a busy street, or cycling past me, Rachel beside him, laughing.

And I hoped, for his sake, that he was right; that he'd somehow managed to find that second chance he so desperately wanted.

But that was one fantasy I couldn't allow into my life, because in my selfishness I'd finally done the unthinkable: I'd destroyed the lives of the two people I loved most. It would be ridiculous to think I deserved another chance and foolishness to believe there was another world with another Rachel. And that she would be waiting for someone like me.

Heart full of sorrow, I posed my ruminations to the stars, to the moon hanging low in the crisp autumn sky.

And I swear that great silver orb seemed to *wink* in response.

THE ROOTS OF LOVE

She heard his voice.

On the hill where she had waited through the years, the hill where he had first declared his love for her, she rustled with anticipation for he had, finally, returned.

And who was he? He was the quick inhaling of crisp, sharp air and the warmth of smouldering cheeks; he was the lightning strike and the smell of burnt copper. A young man of endearing affection who'd gone off to make his fortune in the far, inexplicable world of the city, returning with troubling infrequency to love her, until one day there was nothing left of his love: nothing but the empty wide spaces.

And on the day he did not come back, she wept on that same hill, tears flowing in streams to soak her bare feet, until toes became shoots became roots, fixing her to the soil where their love first grew.

As the seasons turned memories haunted her, memories of times spent lying under spring stars, sitting on a warm summer porch, walking through autumn's kaleidoscope leaves, sleeping by the heart-glow of a winter's fire.

Over the bitter years, she drank the land dry, sucking its sweet water to remind herself of his sweet, wet kisses, until the ground was a hard, barren hill. She survived, then, on the scraps of intermittent rain that pelted the earth, collected in rusted metal canisters which, when full, spilt its contents onto the ground. A taste of metal and stone.

She hated him for lost years, for loneliness, for a life endured.

But as he called her name now, his footsteps scratching across the desolate hill, searching, his voice was heavy with misery and regret. With that, her hatred fled. And when he cried out "I was a fool! Forgive me and be my love once more!" her heart swelled and, in that moment, she longed for him, to hold him fast and close.

And in that brief moment all the lonely, loathsome years passed into obscurity.

But her anguish remained: a stone that would not be moved.

He called her name again.

She reached for him, roots shooting up from the earth, from the soil where their love first grew and dragged him under, pulled him into her, roots twisting and grinding to serrate his flesh and crush his bones.

What Happened to Mrs Eleonora Valdemar, Discovered in a Series of Diary Entries

Excerpts from the remaining pages of this diary have been collected here for the purposes of the Court and are established to have been written between the months of August and October in 1871. The crime scene is twenty miles from Poplar Bluff, Missouri.

<u>August 19th</u>

—seclusion on our remote woodland estate may have taken its toll on me, I duly admit. But I was hardly alone at the time. The boy you hired comes faithfully twice a week to cut wood for the stove or drop off his delivery of vegetables and meats and goes his way without uttering a sound.

Due to your continued lack of response, I no longer see the point in sending you my letters, though I continue to write them, nonetheless. They sit in the drawer of your desk, waiting. Like me. So, I have taken to scribbling in this diary in an attempt to find a home for my many wayward thoughts.

And then there is Amity.

My younger cousin keeps me company, though we do not speak as freely to each other as we once did. Being in the family way does not sit well with her. Since the day my cousin knew she was with child her health took a turn for the worse, and these days she is wracked by a fever that clings to her body. Sometimes I find her lying on the sofa or sitting alone in the kitchen, speaking strange utterances to the air.

I wish I possessed knowledge of the summoning arts and herbal remedies known by the women on her side of the family, stretching down the line and into the past. Women of the dark forest. And maybe if I knew such arts, I could help her, because at one point I feared her condition had worsened, so much so that I almost sent for a doctor.

Almost.

Such recklessness would be unacceptable. The comforts you bestow upon me, dear husband, are more than a woman of my low social standing could have dreamed of, and the education you paid for does not go without appreciation. Therefore, it has always been in my interest to protect your good name. Your ruin is our ruin.

So, what troubles my heart, you may ask, and presses me to continue writing to you with such urgency? Your latest departure for St. Louis, my husband. That is when my fear truly took root.

The strange and unnatural visitor I warned you of? His presence on this haunted land continues to taunt me like a spectral thing born out of some darker realm of existence.

I often see him in the distance, moving between the tangled trees at dusk with surprising agility. I cannot determine any distinguishable features, and if there is a moon her radiance is not overly revealing.

But he is there, I tell you. Every night. Walking our

property. Watching. Maybe even waiting. For what, I do not know. I hardly go outside anymore, and at night I shut and lock every window, every door.

I have taken your Colt repeating handgun out from the closet under the grand staircase and I have loaded it. I now carry the gun with me wherever I go.

Remember, dear husband, I know how to use it. And as the daughter of a backwoodsman of the Ozarks, bred to the dangers of an ancient and unknowable country, I feel safer with it in my hands—

August 30th

—in a rare but welcomed excursion from the house I went out front yesterday to pick lavender that grows by the side of the drive. I find its aroma soothes any troubles the house might hold, and softens its darker edges. It was three o'clock in the afternoon.

The delivery wagon pulled up and in his usual fashion, the urchin boy bid me a silent hello with the tipping of his ragged hat. He dropped off the food parcel, then handed me your letter which announced your return in two months. My initial relief was tinged with cold anticipation.

How long will you stay? Three or four days is usually all you can burden yourself with. You forgot to ask about Amity, about her delicate condition, and not a word was addressed to my welfare. You mentioned nothing of my concern for my unnatural visitor. The grand halls and theatres of St. Louis, and your life there, were all you seem occupied with.

On those rare occasions when you are at home with

me, I always receive the same reply to my queries about the purposes of your trips: business.

Business, you say.

The wind in my ears sounds more like honesty than your excuses. And your apologies, like ghosts, lack substance.

I realised I was alone. The boy and the wagon had gone. I stood with your letter in my closed fist, staring at the bend in the road where the urchin and his wagon must have vanished. The light had long since drained from the sky, leaving me surrounded by cool twilight. Though there was no wind, the tall trees bent at fantastic angles against the sky. The forest undulated as if it were breathing, and the long grasses parted here and there with the movement of some unseen body.

Shaken with the knowledge that I was being watched, I turned to the house to see that all the curtains had been pushed aside and every window was opened. The front door was a gaping maw, exposing the house's murky innards—

September 5th

—though I am at a loss to understand how the house became so open to the elements that day, I cannot blame Amity. Despite her occasional laboured night walks about the house, she rarely leaves her room these days, and I keep the door keys with me at all times. As for unlatching a window, she has never gone against my wishes before, and as she finds it difficult to muster the strength to climb stairs and reach the bedroom windows, I am satisfied she has played no part in this—

September 17th

—there is a drumming at the window behind me.

I sit at the writing desk in your library, pen in hand, steel nib scratching away. Though the sound at the window is persistent an overwhelming sense of dread prevents me from turning around. I fear that to face the one who walks these ancient forests would be to awaken unto myself, to feel the pull of an inhabited reality invisible to our eyes only because we are taught not to recognize its existence.

But what of my visitor's motives? Why does he not burst through a door or smash a window and climb through? And with the house recently found exposed to the elements, God knows he has had his chances to rush inside.

Perhaps he despises ceilings and walls. Perhaps he fears enclosures. If so, is he attempting to lure me out to strike a fatal blow? In my carelessness a few weeks back, while out picking lavender, did I almost fall victim to his dark purpose?

Maybe he is simply trying to drive me mad.

Amity does not react when I announce his presence. She cannot be wholly unaware of the nocturnal mysteries that conspire to torture me, of this I am certain.

The clock strikes nine.

In a moment, I will put the pen down, rise from this chair and walk away, keeping my back to the glass and the primaeval face I know lingers there—

September 23rd

—it was ten o'clock at night when it happened.

Sleep had not come easily, so I decided to walk the

house, checking windows were shut and doors bolted. I was not surprised to find the window at the top of the grand staircase opened. I closed it, though I was certain I had done so previously.

Lamp held high, I made my way to the kitchen. Amity stood at the table, and her eyes were glazed over with fever. She was washing her sweating face in the bucket of well water I had brought in earlier.

I took her arm in an attempt to guide her back to her bedroom, a small pantry just off the kitchen when I was stopped by the skittering of feet outside. It was not unusual for some animals to rummage around the back porch at night.

Thrusting the lamp forward, I moved to the window by the back door to see if I could spy the little creature. There was some moonlight. As I approached, a loud bang came from the door and I jumped back, knocking into the table.

Amity stared at the door and mumbled something obscure.

I was overcome with dread. It was a sinking feeling that, if you failed to return soon, dear husband, we would both die of madness inside these suffocating walls.

Just as I started breathing normally again, a succession of brutal thumps shook the door, one after another, increasing in intensity until I screamed at the vile noise to be gone.

The door shuddered and creaked on its hinges. My cousin moved towards the door. As it did not sit flush with the frame, I could see the door was not locked. I grabbed her arms and pulled her back. With a free hand,

I reached through the side seams of my petticoat, into the pocket, and pulled out the gun.

Silence filled the room.

I waited, holding her and the gun, for how long I cannot tell. She did not try and break free, and I doubt she had the strength to do so if she tried.

I gathered my wits about me enough to let her go. As I did so, I rushed to the door and turned the key. I threw the top bolt across for good measure. As I threw that bolt, I sensed there was a hand pressed against the other side, just inches from my face. Then came a chafing sound: that hand sliding down the outside face of the door. I took a step back. More silence.

Satisfied that he was gone, I guided my cousin back to her bed.

Why did Amity reach for the door? Was her intention to stand exposed so he could rip her and her child from the threshold? Or was Amity simply trying to lock the door, as I had done? I asked her these questions and many more, but she only looked at me strangely, as if I were but a wisp of smoke. I wanted to shake her violently for answers, but I lacked the strength.

What good would it have done? Amity has remained tight-lipped for months, speaking only when some need demanded it. Why should I have expected her to converse with me now? She would no more talk to me than you would come home to be with your wife—

September 25th

—my strange ramblings must provoke you to question my sanity. Sometimes I cannot quite convince myself of what is happening.

Believe me, dear husband, I am well enough in body and mind to know that I am lucid and rational and in control of my faculties.

Is it possible that in her present condition, Amity could be affecting me? I accept that it is, indeed, possible. Those struck with fever have been known to walk about, to carry on conversations with the invisible, to react to ethereal oddities not seen by ordinary human eyes.

And if the visitor is just some abhorrent nightmare on the part of my ailing cousin, then it is conceivable I have been sharing in her reverie through something similar to hysteria, like those poor souls afflicted by *St. Vitus' Dance*, the thousands flailing about in their madness through the streets of Aachen.

Conceivable. But unlikely. For she makes no sound or movement that would induce me into her supposed mania.

So, I must continue to believe the visitor is real, that he is here, and that he is drawn to me.

Or maybe I am, somehow, drawn to him—

October 3rd

—I found myself at the foot of my cousin's bed, gun in hand. She did nothing to indicate she was aware of my presence. She simply lay there, unmoving.

Like me, she is a poor child of this Earth and all its deeper aspects, and that there is some connection between her and my anguish seems reasonable. Would her demise, and that of the child, be the end of my torment? Would my visitor and all the spectral elements of earth and mind, finally, leave me?

It was a strange turn of fate. Strange that I would stop

her from allowing a nameless threat to stand in an opened doorway and yet there I stood, just as much a menace as the thing beyond the door.

Though her delicate condition frustrates me, and her silences irritate me, my heart has always felt affection for my long-suffering cousin.

I lowered the gun.

I was about to leave when she uttered a single word across the darkness between us.

Rawhead.

October 9th

—I remember the story Amity's mother once told us when we were children, before her untimely death. It was a piece of folklore passed on from her mother, and her mother's mother. Of the spectre of a beast, born of blood and suffering, evoked from the sodden earth to feed upon the flesh and bone of the living.

And of Old Betty, the witch of the Ozarks who lived in the dark forest—

October 15th

—every day Amity is closer to delivery.

I was eleven when I helped Mother give birth to my dead brother in our cabin. As usual, Father had gone off on another fur-trapping expedition and would not be back for weeks. When he did return, I took the brunt of his despair for my mother's sake. My dear cousin Amity, his own brother's daughter, was not spared. She was only six years old at the time.

Before he departed on another trip, I made sure he would never harm us again, and the official story is that he disappeared in the forests of Arkansas.

I never told you this because my mother, cousin and I agreed to never speak of it—

—I tell you now, as the day draws ever nearer, that Amity has stopped acknowledging my presence. I would like to believe it is the lingering illness and raging fever that makes her eyes brush past me. But I know there is more to it than that.

And you accepted me as your wife. Was it wrong to expect to be treated as such? Have I displeased you so that you would punish me in such a manner by staying away?

And Amity. My cousin. The young woman who bears *your* child. What will become of her?

What will become of us all?

October 19th

—after inspecting the house last night, I went into the sitting room to close the curtains. Before I could pull them against the moonlight, I caught sight of my thin reflection in the glass.

I tell you truthfully, the face there resembled mine in every detail, except the eyes, dear husband, the eyes. They did not stare back at me but considered me with deep interest, and with a look I knew contained an infallible truth: that an ancient and familiar hand had laid itself upon me and was somehow calling to me.

Chilled by such a garish idea I turned away from my ghostly double. When I looked back to the window he was out there, my mysterious visitor, standing at the edge of the shadowed tree line several yards away in the grass. How long had he been there looking at me I do not know.

In a fit of madness, I unlatched and threw up the window. I called to him, shouted at him, implored him to be gone, to return to where he came from. I felt my skirts part and the gun was in my hand. I fired into the night. Two shots.

A cloud must have passed in front of the moon for the yard was thrown into darkness. When the light returned, my visitor was gone.

I scurried through the house, double-checking the locks on the windows and doors—

October 23rd

—now I remember the creature Rawhead was once a razorback boar and companion to Old Betty. When she had heard the boar had been killed by a brazen hunter, a man whose blood was full of arrogance and pride, the old woman went mad with grief and summoned more than just the animal's spirit to seek vengeance and placate her anguished heart.

What returned was a form that walked upright, somewhat like a man, and whose head was a boar's skull, stripped of its skin and bathed in blood.

The beast stalked the night lands in want of the man's conceited flesh—

October 27th

—I awoke with a convulsion of arms and legs. It was as if something called to me while I slumbered.

Overwhelmed with a terror I could not explain, I fumbled in the dark until I found the bedside table. Striking a match, I lit the oil lamp and plunged down the corridor, down the back staircase to the kitchen and Amity's room. I threw open the door and stumbled in, holding the lamp out ahead of me, its yellow light reaching into the dark.

The bed was empty.

At the front of the house, I found the great oak door thrown open. Outside was a full moon, and its radiance spilt through the corridor, stretching shadows to dark corners.

And silhouetted against the moonlight was Amity. One hand lay against the doorframe, the other arm was wrapped across her swollen stomach.

I put the lamp down and leapt to her side. She turned to look at me. The white nightdress was wet between her thighs, and a glistening liquid covered the floorboards beneath her.

The time had come.

She slid down the doorframe and lay across the threshold, the lower half of her body outside on the cold stones. As much as I tried, I could not lift her and drag her back into the house. Throughout her labour, Amity never looked at me but gritted her teeth and fixed her dark eyes upon the sky in silent anger.

There was blood everywhere, on her nightdress, on the stones between her legs, and on the step beneath us. As I got down on my knees to receive the child, hands drenched in gore, my poor cousin let out her first and only cry, a tormented sound imbued with loathing and malice, then fell back upon the stones and died.

And in my arms, I held the newborn. Your daughter.

I did not need to turn my head to know my visitor was there, standing at my shoulder. Rawhead. He smelled of damp earth and his queer utterances were deep whispers from the back of a cave.

Oddly, my heart did not leap in distress. The fear that had once burdened me did not manifest itself. Maybe the beast had picked up a scent of familiarity upon my skin or in my blood. A scent that tied me to my cousin, the great-great-granddaughter of his master. Old Betty of the dark forest.

Still on my knees, I wiped the screaming child clean with my nightdress.

Rawhead's arms stretched out toward me, large fingers splayed.

I quickly glanced at him. Shimmering yellow eyes in a razorback's bloodied hogshead blinked at me. The hair rose from his back and shoulders, glistening in the moonlight.

I gazed hard at my cousin's corpse, growing cold upon the stones. I looked at the squirming infant. The child was the seed of your contemptuous conduct. Amity's dead flesh was the outcome.

So, I asked myself, would you mourn my cousin? And when you returned would you look upon the child, cherish her, and claim her as your own? Would you teach her your manners and customs, as you had done for me?

And if so, tell me, husband, would you deem the child acceptable to present to the members of your polite society? Or will she also come to know the pain and humiliation of your long absences?

On these questions, I did not linger.

I gave the beast Rawhead the howling child.

Holding your daughter close, he made for the wilderness, disappearing as though slipping behind a black curtain.

It started to rain—

October 29th

—the darkness is deep, and the stars are gone.

Your house lies open, windows, and doors, all thrown wide. I no longer wish to seal myself inside. And I now know that I never wanted to.

Leaves float in and settle on the furniture and the floors, and the scent of damp earth fills the house. Small woodland animals skurry in the kitchen, wrestling for what food is left. At my request, the boy you hired no longer comes. Crows perch on windowsills, silent, watching.

What of my cousin? I buried her at the edge of the forest. You will see a wooden marker there.

And I have not seen the beast Rawhead again.

So, unrestricted by time or our misplaced lives, I sit here at your desk waiting for the hour when your carriage will stop outside the front door, as it has always done. You will disembark, and walk carefully across the pebbles to the stone step. You will come through the front door and into your once warm and comfortable home. You will find me in the library.

And when that moment comes, I will stop scratching away in this diary, put down the pen and turn to you, fingers clasping the handgun you once kept in the closet under the stairs.

I feel safer with it in my hands—

THE STARS MUST WAIT

The year 2024 was the centennial anniversary of the publication of Yevgeny Zamyatin's classic story, <u>We</u>. To celebrate such a milestone, this story was written and takes place several decades after the end of that novel.

The old house is an antediluvian corpse, silent, tomblike, alone with its rotting innards of antiquities from a dead era. Unlike the Ancient House inside the protection of One-State this ruin, as with other Mephi ruins, sits *outside* the Wall. Outside comfort and safety. Outside normality.

The difference between them is the house inside our beloved domed metropolis serves as a repository for old-world items taken from archaeological sites. This old house is just a ruin.

I walk through the house, pistol raised but find no other enemies. No Mephi. No deviant Numbers.

I head back into the mess of what I assume is a communal room, where I step around the child's dead mother—a bullet hole in her forehead. Three Unit members come down the stairs and give me the "all-clear" sign, then exit the house.

"Secured," I say to Constable K-121.

She holds a feral child by the arm. A girl, two, maybe three years old. Once in a nursery and later a reconditioning centre, the child will learn how to live in our society, like the others we have taken.

"That makes seven ferals today," K-121 says. "We've done better." She nods to the whimpering child. "I'll take her outside."

K-121 leads the child out to where the eighteen members of Unit 65 stand watch.

In this moment of quiet, my mind wants to take in my surroundings: paintings, a brass statue of a bull, green with age, a musical instrument, and a bookshelf. My eyes are drawn to the stained-glass window across the room, pastoral and oozing tranquillity: a hill, bathed in glorious light. The heat of the sun bursts through the coloured glass, embracing me.

On a table, a book of cracked, black leather. The gold wording, still bright, tells me it's a book of theological doctrine. (The language is archaic but similar enough to our own that I can make out the meaning.)

I flip through its gilded pages and stop at a passage proclaiming a deific plan to 'give hope and a future'. I scoff. We Numbers know the plans One State has for us. Formulae and reason secure our present and create our future. Hope, an abstract, has nothing to do with it.

And yet, some of our own embrace abstraction.

And violence.

Why do the Mephi treasure these things? And what about them corrupts a Number, turns them into deviants?

I think of A-505. Hand in my coat pocket, I stroke the ancient ivory brooch he gifted me, and wonder why I carry it around.

"What is it about these old places" —I jerk around at

K-121's voice— "that turns some of our own against us?" Her smile is barely perceptible. "Apologies, I've startled you."

"I'm fine," I say stiffly.

"You seem distracted." She furrows her brows. "Maybe it was too soon to return to duty. A concussion is a serious matter."

"I'm fine." I collect myself. "But I don't have an answer to your question."

"How many of us will be exposed to flawed logic, become intellectually compromised, become deviants, before we see victory over the Mephi? Dealing with the tribes is hard enough, but having to deal with turncoats in our society—"

She's rightfully worried, but who wouldn't be when columns of our citizens want to unite us with the Mephi, drag us beyond the dome, beyond the Wall, and into chaos?

"Victory against the Mephi," she says, "against the corruption of Numbers, is paramount if we're to take our methods to other worlds."

"We have reason and scientific rigour on our side," I say. "And a Benefactor who guides us."

"So, we do," she says and exits the ruin.

As we begin the trek back to One State, I steal a glance back at the old structure. I try to imagine a past that created this house of flotsam, and the madness of those who admired freedom of expression, of those who conjured up philosophies and theosophical insights—freedom, creativity, spirits, demons, gods—all without the security of scientific and numerical management.

The Mephi cling to their old convictions. They exist beyond the Wall, trusting they are richer in body and mind than we could ever be, leading more fulfilling lives than we could ever know.

Or so they believe.

*

A-505 is lounging on the settee when I arrive home.

"How did you get in here? What if *they're* watching?"

"Your Bureau of Guardians?" He shrugs. "I suspect they have bigger things to worry about. The Wall, for instance."

Numerous times we've rebuilt sections of the Wall after the Mephi broke through. The most recent attack left large segments severely damaged. Repairs are ongoing.

I draw the curtains across my translucent walls, even though it's not Sex Day and I don't have permission to do so. "You can't show up whenever you wish."

He holds up a visitation card. "I'm assigned to visit you today. Didn't you get the memo?"

A forgery, of course. The Table of approved movements is rarely changed without justification. I still have my sidearm. I could hold him here and call for backup. He knows this. He also knows I can't bring myself to do it.

"Don't remember?" he says. "Guess that blow to the head really did mess with your brain."

Five weeks ago, my Unit was ambushed on the third floor of an abandoned factory by a group of Mephi. We had to shoot our way out. K-121 told me that on the second floor, an explosion threw me against a concrete wall. All I recall is touching the side of my head and my hand coming away, sticky with blood.

"First K-121, now you." I clench my fists. "You think I'm unfit for duty?"

"Well, I guess if the doctors were happy to release you—"

"Get to the point."

"Bring in a hefty load of Mephi young today?" he says.

"And once reconditioned, they'll be productive Numbers. Unlike you."

"Conquer the Mephi and stop the conflict by absorbing their offspring. Will that work?"

"The probability the war will end more quickly as a result of Mephi assimilation is high enough to make it a viable option."

"Probability," he says. "Not certainty? Since when did the State see chance as an acceptable mode of operation?" He shakes his head. "Chance, they tell us, is like the square root of minus one. Both are imaginary."

"You embrace imaginary things." My voice is curdled milk.

"Even if you take every child and end the Mephi as a culture, you'll find you still have a deviant problem."

"Are you here to insult me and criticise State policy?"

"No," he says. "J-800 was executed by The Machine yesterday. Just curious how that makes you feel."

My chest burns at the mention of that Number.

"Do you think she should've received The Operation?"

I ask. "She was more than compromised and deserved more than psychosurgery."

"Well, I suppose I'd also prefer The Machine over being purged of emotion and the ability to innovate. Oh, don't look shocked. Would you rather be moulded into a state of mechanical reliability? To become nothing more and nothing less than a human tractor?"

"She was a deviant."

"Behind closed doors, she called herself Olga."

"And what Mephi name do you call yourself?"

He flashed a crooked smile.

"J-800 was supplying weapons to the Mephi," I say, "and the Benefactor could make only one decision."

"But you turned her in," he says. "And there's more to your decision to hand her over than you let on."

I bristle at the suggestion I could be so influenced by love or jealousy—old-world concepts. I'm a Number. A product of reasoning, scientific rigour.

"We were tasked to offer the State new life," I say. "*We*. You and me. Numerically matched by a meticulously composed equation to take part in the birthing mandate. But you chose to disregard mathematical truth, exposing yourself to a deviant."

"How did it feel?" he presses me. "Was it satisfying, acting on scorn and jealousy instead of reason?"

"Your actions put you on the other side of all we hold true. What happened to you?"

"You tell me. I'm not doing your job for you."

"Speaking of jobs, I hear you've been put on Work Leave from the construction of the new *Integral*."

"Ah," he says, as if remembering something forgotten.

"That instrument to carry the Benefactor's wisdom to the stars." He shrugs. "My production was down—apparently. Lack of focus due to exhaustion, or something like that."

"You're compromised. That much is clear."

He waves a hand, dismissively. "If you wish to believe that, so be it."

"Nothing is a matter of belief."

"And yet the Mephi live by it," he says. "Look, if I'm compromised I'm in the first phase before becoming a deviant. I need reconditioning before that happens. Save me. Turn me in."

I'm silent.

He clicks his tongue. "As an agent, you really should be able to make that decision. Here, I'll make it easy for you." He picks up the phone and holds it out to me. "Take it. Dial your colleagues."

I put my hand out but stopped short of grabbing the phone.

"It's every Number's solemn duty to preserve the truth of the State," he says.

When I find my voice, it's small and weak in my ears.

"Get out."

He grins and puts the phone down.

As I watch him head for the door, a question rears up in my mind, one I've resisted asking him. "Are you also supplying weapons to the Mephi?"

"What does the math tell you?" he says and shuts the door.

*

The conflict with the Mephi started before I was born. The Operation was mandated for all Numbers to stave off the psychosis and the riots the war created. But the new Benefactor rescinded that directive, and with new formulae reasoned a more aggressive reconditioning for every Number would help reduce the numbers of citizens being compromised and support the State's foundations. An increase in births would bolster our population, securing our future.

The Assimilation Programme for Mephi young was part of that reasoning.

*

Early morning. An execution in the State Square. Every Number is required to observe. The Square is packed. The rest of the population watches on large screens hung on every street corner.

In the Square, I stand with K-121 and other agents near the back of a crowd of uniformed Numbers. They are a sea, one great body moving in rhythmic waves before a massive stage.

Six deviants are brought up, and a voice from the tannoy cries:

> "Those who seek to destroy us from within,
> tear us from logic and reason, will never
> prevail.
> We thrive because our lives are regulated,
> scientifically operated; we've reached beyond
> the uncertainty of the old world. Where chaos
> once ruled, the State has brought order; where
> the calamity of desperate ideas kept us apart,
> the State has produced a unity of minds by way of
> formulae, equations whose solutions are fixed
> within the logic of mathematics—"

A cheer goes up from the crowd.

"—*only logic and reason and the purity of numbers can carry us toward that ideal life.*"

As the six are led to The Machine, State music is played, chromatic scales meet, separate, and are dissected by Frauenhofer lines in a regular, repeating pattern. Order against chaos.

A-505 is two rows ahead and to my left. I stare at him, hard, willing him to look over at me. A futile exercise.

Love.

Jealousy.

The numerator and denominator of the same fraction—bitterness.

*

The executions are supposed to uplift and bind us to a common cause. But they're not the salve I need to squash my desire to understand what happened to A-505 to make him turn his back on his duty, to turn his back on me.

Why am I so insistent on knowing the answer?

I baulk at the idea I could be compromised. But how else can I explain my lack of focus, my jumbled thoughts, my emotionalism? Turning myself in means losing my place in the Bureau if I do. Years of starting over.

If I'm compromised, there'll be no escaping the remedy: reconditioning.

And if I wait too long to seek help, I may be too far gone; then it's The Operation. Psychosurgery.

I don't want to be a human tractor.

In the shower, the urge to scream. I shove a washcloth into my mouth to muffle the sound.

*

Another mission outside the Wall. Remnants of a street, and a row of dilapidated houses in what was once a cul-de-sac. The forest has reclaimed most of the roofless homes, trees grow out of holes like mouths that were once windows, and vines creep over exterior walls.

K-121 takes half the team, spreads out, and checks the houses on the other side of the broken street.

Shots break out.

"That didn't take long," I mutter. A door off its hinges, leans against a tree. I hide under it.

"Anyone have visual contact!" K-121 barks.

A barrage of "*Negative*" from the team.

Our enemies are everyone and nowhere. If ghosts are real, they'd be Mephi.

"Numbers 15, 320, 670 and 675," K-121 calls out. "Watch our backs. Don't let them surround us."

Ahead, movement. Bushes rustle between houses. "End of the road. Cover me!" I make a break for it.

Down on my haunches, I push through the bushes to the other side and look straight into the eyes of a boy, hiding in the brush a metre from my face. There are others just over his shoulder, all staring out at me. Five Mephi young.

I'm frozen there, oblivious to the bedlam in the street on the other side of the houses.

The child takes a step back; the others do the same.

The Mephi attack is a simple tactic to buy time so their young can escape us.

They boy takes another step back; so do the others, again and again. I watch them disappear.

K-121 bursts through the bushes. "Are you okay?"

I get to my feet. "I'm fine."

"What was back here?" She peers into the dense foliage.

"Nothing."

"You came back here for nothing?"

I leave her standing there.

*

I froze!

I've never froze before.

Five feral young got away, and I'm responsible.

Luckily, K-121 doesn't question me further.

*

Evening is a warm band of light, filtering through the window into my office. But the comfort it offers diminishes with the onslaught of night, and I'm left with the chill of uncertainty and self-doubt.

The stars shine through the State's translucent dome, a reminder of our objective: to carry our way of life out there and end the struggles other worlds endure. To save them from themselves.

How can I serve such a noble purpose as I am?

"D-83?"

I jump. "Sorry, Constable. Didn't hear you come in."

"Your shift's over."

I look at the wall clock. Over an hour and I haven't begun. "I'm still trying to write this report on the incident today."

"You won't get it done staring out the window."

"I'll just file the report and go home."

Her brow furrows and there's a small tilt of her head. She's evaluating me, as any good Number would.

"You're off Table."

I do my best to look firm, unmoved by her tone.

"I'm never late with my reports, Constable."

"Nonetheless, it'll have to wait."

Her gaze is a steel wall. I need to choose my battles wisely.

"You're right." I grab my coat. "Thank you for putting me straight."

"D-83." She stops me. "A medical has been arranged for you tomorrow morning. A follow-up, as a precaution. We need to be sure you are, in fact, in top shape to continue your duties."

*

I pass the medical. Again. I don't know how.

If I were Mephi, I'd call it a miracle.

*

I'm Tabled for a walk this evening. I make my way to the eastern Promenade, a raised stretch of concrete, overlooking the city centre below. I stop to gaze down into the heart of the State.

A man sidles up to me. "I'd heard about the attack. I would've come to see you, but I know you wouldn't have appreciated that."

"You're everywhere, A-505," I mutter. "In my home, in my head, on my walk. Can I ever be rid of you?"

"I haven't corrupted you if that's what you're suggesting. You've been sleepwalking in a static dream, D-83, and you've woken up all on your own. You're thinking beyond formulae now."

"I've been awake all my life." I scoff. "Being awake is to be a Number, part of something managed, structured, bigger than myself."

He sighs. "A fault in the State's thinking is the fact that Numbers *can* be compromised."

"A biological machine is like any artificial machine; we can break down internally, or we're damaged by an outside source."

"How you can be so black and white, so cold, despite all that's happened, all you've learned?"

"Learned?" I shoot back. "About what? What it's like to be unable to control myself and my thoughts? Confusion? Anxiety? Being unable to focus?"

"Lower your voice. You're creating a scene."

I feel the prick of many eyes. Numbers pass us, staring, whispering. The heat of shame pools in my stomach.

"What about J-800?" I whisper. "Did she know about the attack that injured me? Was it planned?" I turn to stare at the side of his face. "Did you know about it?"

"I wasn't privy to everything they discussed."

"I could've been killed."

"If your life was at risk, and if I knew anything, I would've told you. Believe me."

"Why should I? You didn't tell me you'd turned down pairing with me. I found out through the doctors."

He mumbles something. I avert my eyes and look out at the lights of the State, burning bright and hard against the night.

"And our matching?" I say. "Did J-800 persuade you to refuse it? Or did you make that decision all by yourself?"

No answer. He's gone.

*

Nights have been mostly sleepless. My head swirls constantly, jumbled thoughts, ideas, emotions. Rage. Jealousy. Love. Anger. The memory of the tranquillity from the stained-glass window, its warmth, seems to calm me, so I try to hold on to that.

Okay, so I can't turn him in. I'm attached to him beyond reason, though he can't be saved.

But I can save myself. I can turn myself in. I should. I must.

That idea—and its consequences—keeps me awake even longer.

*

The next day, there's an explosion inside the State. A tanker filled with fuel for the *Integral*. It was driven straight into a reconditioning centre. A suicide run.

Deviants? Or Mephi who managed to slip into the State?

Far in the distance is a thin, black thread of smoke, twisting up into the sky.

The Bureau Superior convenes an emergency meeting of all Units. I won't attend. I walk home.

In my bathroom mirror, I fail to recognise my reflection. Everything I am—loyal Number, disciplined, dedicated agent of the State, all of me—seems like the pieces of another person.

I stand there, staring at the stranger in the glass.

*

My phone rings.

"Don't worry." It's A-505. The line crackles. "I wouldn't call you on a monitored line. I'm down in the abandoned switchboard centre, using an old cable. I wanted to let you know I'm leaving."

"Leaving? For where?"

"Anywhere away from the State. I can't stay here. That explosion has put attention on my associates, and by default, me."

My mind goes strangely quiet. One idea dominates. I've made up my mind. Strangely, I feel at peace. My thoughts have been filled with chaos, and my daily life is full of insecurity. Starting over is the only reasonable option. I need to operate at full capacity. The State is depending on me. I need scientific management embedded in my life once more, to be immersed in it, and guided by it. I need to clear my mind of distractions.

I need the formulaic rhythm of purpose.

The purpose of the State.

"You can come with me," he says.

His offer horrifies me.

"I'm turning myself in," I say. "For reconditioning."

"Why do that?"

"Because I'm a Number, that's why."

A pause. "Of course."

The line crackles.

"Before you make that your final decision," he says, "I want you to know something. The *Integral*. They've done something to it, changed something…"

"Changed what? Who's 'they'?"

The line crackles again. "…discovered a peculiar

metal-cased object in the repository, sitting among the other debris..." —*crackle*— "the *Integral* now carries it...an old-world terror..."

"What are you talking about?"

"...there could be empty lands beyond the realm of the Mephi. It may be safe there."

"The line is bad. Can you repeat?"

He doesn't hear me.

"It must've..." —*crackle*— "...doubt the Benefactor is aware..." —*crackle*— "Whatever's going on, whatever's being planned, it's coming from inside..." —*crackle*—

"Say that again?"

The line goes dead.

*

A-505. Was he apprehended? Did he make it out?

And me? I'll stick to my plan and turn myself in. But first, I'm compelled to do something, something that's without reason.

Tomorrow is a Tabled personal day.

I'm going back to that house.

*

I stand before the stained-glass window. It presides over the room, a bright and golden window that baths me in its illumination, its warmth smothering me. It's fallacious in its reassurance for its comfort is fleeting. This place, these things, A-505 himself, offer nothing. I know that now. And I'm ready to do what's necessary. For the State and me.

I grab a brick and throw it. The shattering of glass is a cleansing music.

I stuff the fireplace with wood, broken chairs, table legs anything that will burn. I grab the black leather-bound book, too, a book of an unknown, nonsensical god, a god who never innovated or invented anything other than confusion. Not a rational, working god at all, not a god who is predictable, and reliable. I throw it in the fireplace.

I strike a match, set it all ablaze, and watch it burn. I want it to burn away the confusion, the uncertainty, all the things that threatened my life's purpose.

I finger the brooch, a reminder of A-505 and all the lost things of that old world that deserved to be lost. I throw it on the fire.

"I thought you might return here," 121's voice is ice water poured down my back. "This is where it all came undone for you. Defeated by a corrupted Number and pieces of coloured glass."

I keep my back to her. "I'm going to turn myself in."

"Admirable."

I turn. "You must've been aware that I've been compromised for some time."

"Long enough." She points her gun at me. "Your sidearm. Toss it away, slowly."

I throw it across the room.

"What of A-505?" I ask.

"The fool was dangerous, but he served our purposes." She smiles wryly.

"Purposes? Where is he now?"

"He's eluded us for the for the moment," she says.

A part of me is relieved; another part is sad that he refuses to be saved.

"We'd suspected him of being compromised and had been watching him for some time," she says. "We arranged your matching, knowing it would fail because of his dedication to J-800, to her associates and their cause."

"You arranged that? Why?"

"To see how you'd react, of course. Especially once you found out who he was spending time with. We needed to see how the old evils of love, jealousy and anger played out in you. I must say, you came undone faster than I thought you would."

"The Bureau was testing my loyalties?"

"No." She takes a step forward. The floorboards groan. "We were."

"And who are 'we'?"

"A cabal of agents who've studied the edicts of the Benefactor and determined the State to be insufficiently guided. The programme must end, the Mephi youth purged from our society, and every Number subjected to The Operation. We must return to the first path set out for us."

"Human tractors? Every Number?" I recoil. "Without innovation, the State can't hope to continue its march towards perfection. One reason the Benefactor rescinded the old order."

"I concede the point, and to address that problem we will reserve innovation for ourselves. We will direct the State from here on."

"And the Benefactor?"

"She's been deposed. Last night." She shrugs at my shock. "A conflict was inevitable. All agents who resist us will be eliminated."

A-505 said that what was being planned came from *inside.*

"A coup, K-121? How very old world."

"A mathematical necessity," she snaps. "It's been stalemate after stalemate for years. And yes, a stalemate is a failure because you're still failing to win. We have The Operation. And we now have the means to deal with the Mephi threat outside the Wall."

"What does that mean?"

Her face is steel. "You'll return with me. In this delicate time, you must be presented to the Numbers and made an example. You are, after all, a product of the Benefactor's failure."

"I've committed no violence," I say. "I'm not a deviant."

"You're worse than that, D-83," she says. "You're Mephi."

*

Mephi? My head reels.

"You were found in a place like this," she continues, "with many windows similar to that one, and many black books. They called it a house of worship. Don't you see? Your *memories* brought you here."

"I don't remember anything."

"Buried memories, repressed trauma, can influence without being fully surfaced. One develops a distorted view of life, the world, and develops an illusionary perception of self."

My distractions, emotion not tempered by reason, the inability to follow State norms and turn A-505 in...

"The brooch?" she says. "It was in your file. It belonged to your mother. We arranged for A-505 to get hold of it and return it to you as part of our strategy, a first step in opening your mind; the first step in finding out how suppressed your original self truly was."

She takes a step closer.

"And you know what we've learned? You can't fight the mind. That's why The Operation is such a valuable tool."

"Lies!"

"Come now. What purpose would it serve to lie?"

"I'm a Number. I'm D-83."

Another step closer, until she's looking me dead in the eyes. "You'll *never* be one of us."

My fury is shrapnel flying in all directions. I don't recall what happened, but when I regain my faculties K-121 is crumpled on the floor, making small noises, trying to lift herself.

I dislodge a stack of burning chairs from the pile on the hearth. The fire spreads quickly.

*

I leave the house behind.

All my emotion is gone.

Is this what it's like after The Operation? To be numb and walking with the purpose of a machine?

I come to a plain of soft green grass, with the State in the far distance. Columns of black smoke, the smoke of riots and madness, rising high above the buildings under the dome.

I watch the State burn, burn as K-121 did, burn like the house, with all its ancient, primaeval flotsam of philosophy and religion and free-thinking and selfish desires—the things A-505 and his ilk admired. Everything burning.

A mother. A child. Numbers and Mephi. The State and the natural world. Inside and Outside. Chaos and order. Reason and belief.

"I am D-83," I repeat this to the trees, the birds chittering overhead.

A single column of white smoke rises from behind the State, climbing over the dome. Something long and metallic, like a needle stitching a white line up the sky.

The *Integral*.

K-121's words echo in my head: *"And we now have the means to deal with the Mephi threat outside the Wall."*

How did A-505 describe it?

A metal-cased object. An old-world terror.

Of course. When victory is paramount, the stars must wait.

Sitting on the grass, I recite the words that had come over the tannoy, words clear and full of purpose:

"...we thrive because our lives are regulated" —I say it to the grass, to the sun fading behind the smouldering city, and the warm colours, oozing tranquillity, blooming across the western sky— "where chaos once ruled, the State has brought order; where the calamity of disparate ideas kept us apart, the State has brought unity of mind by way of formulae, equations whose solutions remain fixed within the logic of numbers."

The *Integral* stops climbing, arches, and begins its descent; the white line stitching a path toward the earth, pulling down the sky.

I think of A-505. I'd like to think he made it, that he's safe in some far land.

"...it is only logic and reason and the purity of numbers," I mutter, "that can carry us toward the ideal state of being."

Or so we believe.

There's an intense pulse, a flash, and the world is bathed in glorious light.

THE CLARITY OF ICE

I.

I gripped the interface with heated disgust. Synapses were breaking down, some were shifting their pulse rhythms, while others were stuck in flux; millions upon millions of nanos were running around, clueless, as if zapped by a heavy dose of the stupids.

I couldn't understand it: the rooting into the surrounding ecosystem had been flawless, the bio-programmers for Beta habitat integrated into the surroundings and coaxed by their artificial programmers to grow perfect, natural habitats, enclosed and self-sufficient. It had been a textbook performance.

Then why are you collapsing? I chided the static-ridden threshold. *Why?*

I writhed in my seat in the control bubble of the landing bug and seethed at the decay of my systems control ganglia. My program buoy shuddered. Algorithms manifested themselves and scattered past me like so many dead leaves on a Veronian wind. The massive tangle of information before me struck a discordant note.

From the command shuttle in orbit, Cruz des-Manas, senior bio-farmer and planetfall coordinator on this seeding run, was overseeing cross-checks on the System Platform's induction flow and stabilisation subroutines. I saw her in the digiscape distance. She appeared as an octopus whose many tentacles flickered about at what looked like a swarm of large black flies. Beta was collapsing in upon itself.

"Systems are shutting down all over," I said.

"Yeah, so tell me something new," she shot back.

"*Bitch!*" I muttered between my teeth; ears loaded with the system's incoherent babbling.

"Keep your eyes open, Karlyn. I suspect this may cause the nodules' systems to panic and self-isolate."

"Shit, now my program buoy is sinking." I had sent out for a pattern trace to find the culprit but all I got was a whole lot of nothing.

"Organiform supports are dying," Cruz announced, there was an edge in her voice. "Just as I suspected, the system's grids for the nodules have locked themselves tight. The seeding protocol has shut down. At least the final coding sequence for the nodules hasn't started."

"I'm cutting contact with Beta. The feedback is damaging our systems."

As I prepared to invoke the nanocrobe buffers to coat and isolate the undamaged programmers, a lightning crack ruptured the digisky. Beta Platform, whose garbled double-speak dominated most of my channels, howled and discharged a burst of static.

With quick efficiency, my biolastic suit's response mode kicked in. A silver screen went up, caught the burst, amplified it, and sent it right back to the Platform. There was a shower of blue-white particles, a wrenching noise that threatened to shatter my ears, and I was thrown clear. The digivisor on my interface pulled back like melting plastic and withered.

I sat in my organiform chair, head aching, and cursed Beta's bloody haemoglobular flow.

"Total systems shutdown," said Cruz. "We're dead here."

My suit was peeling, the heat from the breakdown burning my skin. I managed to pull it off, and it crinkled up on the floor and turned from metallic grey to deep black.

"The overload burst got through to my buoy, Cruz, and disintegrated my interface suit. I got fucking fried."

"We need a full systems check," she said.

"I'm fine, thanks for asking." I sat back down, careful of my burns. Not exactly the response I was looking for. But then, what did I expect? I grunted (*intolerable little shit!*) and wondered what the hell I ever saw in her.

"Any damage to the bug?" she said. "I can't get a full connection to the lander right now. A few of my ancillary systems are down."

I checked the lander's readouts. "Affected systems have automatically rerouted themselves, except aspects of my life support. I got air and pressure, but the heating is minimal, so it'll get cold in here tonight. At least this thing can still fly." I grabbed a tube of gel from the first aid kit under the seat and rubbed it on my burns. "But it's not the bug I'm worried about."

Were the seed-colonists for the drop unharmed? It had taken over sixteen system fly-bys to find a suitable host-planet this time, one with enough of a vibrant eco-system from which our nanos could grow the living habitats, like the reconstruction couch reinforces my body's bone structure for work, ground side. It was the longest gap between seeding runs we had experienced for years. Naturally, when the sample drone returned with a positive result, we were all eager to get to work.

How did I end up with Cruz on this assignment? We didn't get to choose who we worked with, of course. The rota was the rota.

"The organiform nodules could be undamaged," she said. "No way of telling unless you can reopen their control grids. We won't get authorisation to save the stock if we can't verify its authenticity."

Cruz had never lost human stock before. *Not ever.* Never lost a Platform, for that matter. She had an innate ability for biotech, a natural talent. She had even improved upon some of the coding for the Platforms. She was the best, a shining star among those like us, the few who made it Above.

As far as my situation was concerned, it was my final assignment before being promoted to senior farmer and planetfall coordinator. I would be Cruz's equal. I had worked hard all my life, made sacrifices, and done everything required of me. I had made it to where I needed to be, done what Mother Moira had failed to do.

Through the viewport, the surroundings became hazy in the winter's evening light; frost formed quickly over the viewport, a thin, crisp sheen of ice. The effect warped the view outside, and things appeared milky, distant and unclear.

"Whatever happened," she added, "must be very specific if it can take down the entire Platform and make the control grids go into lockdown. We'll need to be meticulous when going through the data. Luckily, all information up until the incident is secured."

"Technical errors don't cause the type of problems we've just experienced," I said.

"Well, it seems we've got a new kind of technical problem. Unless you got any other ideas?"

I looked at Cruz through the vid-cam. She looked at me and furrowed her brows.

"What?" she said. "Sabotage?"

"It's possible." It was a long shot. The farming systems were under such tight surveillance, and the programmers kept changing, rotating and upgrading the fail-safes two or three times a day. It was harder to sneak around, hitching rides on the many undercurrents of the Ring Ship's systems, than it used to be. But that was the only explanation I could come up with at the time.

"A contaminant?"

I shrugged. "Someone must've dropped a bomb on us. It's the only thing that makes sense."

She scowled and shook her head. "If a person was good enough to get past all the security and plant their poison to spoil the coding, then they'd be good enough to cover their tracks."

"Possibly. Every system has a weakness, Cruz. Every movement leaves some residue, somewhere."

"But would it be enough to lead the Ring's security programmers to the source? Even if they managed to track someone down to a section within the Ring, well, it's a mighty big ship to not have precise coordinates to zero in on a saboteur."

Our ship was a massive, spinning ring, nine-hundred and forty kilometres in diameter, connected by spokes to a central hub and drive system—a lot of territory for the authorities to comb over. Not impossible, just difficult.

"If you're right," she said. "If it was a saboteur, our best bet from here is to focus on a contaminant, which will leave traces behind."

"What if the saboteur had insider assistance?" I said, excited she would even entertain my idea. "A contact on the security team. That's an area to pursue."

An alarm howled and died.

"*Shit!* Can't pursue anything at the moment," Cruz said. "Long-range comms link just went down. We're cut off from the Ring."

"Cut off?"

"Yes, cut off," she barked. "That's not so difficult to understand, is it?"

I could just detect a tinge of panic at the back of her throat. "How much do they know about what happened?"

"Enough to know we're dead in the water."

Another alarm sounded. The image became grainy and then cleared.

"A few more systems are gone," she said. "Just lost the long-range data beams and there's a flutter in the main drive system."

Shit was going from disaster to full-on nightmare.

II.

I am from Below. The outer ring of the ship. The very bottom. I was not born into privilege. Nothing has ever been handed to me, no doors opened, no pathways cleared. I languished in one-third gravity, as my forbearers before me. Opportunity is for those Above, up the spokes from the outer ring to the central habitats of the free-floaters, the Zero-G Apostles, the ones who scatter life throughout the universe and believe it their Elysian right to do so. (And if one day the seedlings grow to break gravity, maybe some of them could aspire to be apostles, too.)

Of course, they deny any assertion of elitist conceits, with slogans like, 'Get a high enough end-of-cycle communal credit assessment!' or 'Want to progress? Follow the rules, check your behaviour, and get a bonus!'.

Just words. Nothing more.

Few make it Above, of course, but just enough to give hope to the rest of us.

When I was a child, Mother Moira made it through her fifth assessment, but it was meagre, only enough to push her up from low-level administrator to junior civil servant in our local district. Though the amount would not lift us from Below, as she had dreamed and hoped and prayed, we would be able to live in a slightly better district, with access to slightly better accommodation and medical treatment.

Not a life, but a slightly better existence.

After a time she could, of course, try again. But even as a child, simply looking at her, I knew how unlikely that would be. She had lost something of herself, her spark, her quick wit, her laugh—everything I knew about Mother Moira seemed to have abandoned her. "Put in a good showing, Karlyn. Give it all you've got. That's how they'll notice you, and you'll earn their respect." Those words she had drilled into me dried up and no longer fell from her lips. For the next few years, not much came out of her mouth at all.

I found her on the settee one morning. Pale. Cold. Eyes dull and looking toward oblivion. She had succumbed to whatever recreational drugs I knew she had been taking at the time.

Throughout my schooling, I lived with various members of the community. Eventually, my grief turned to resentment. How could she let herself waste away? So much for her high and mighty words…

Since I was a minor and an orphan, her communal credits were applied to me, yet I was not allowed to apply them to those who had taken me in, to show gratitude. You're not allowed to increase the amount of someone else's pot. That's cheating the system.

I let the credits stack up and resisted the urge to cash them in on the small pleasures they could open for me. Somehow, I drew the attention of the Junior Lottery. Maybe it was the amount I stored up. Maybe it was my high academic grades. But my name was drawn. I would be lifted Above. I would access the highest levels of education and practical training, as well as some of the most distinguished sectors of work available up there. A silent benefactor would apply additional credits to see me through.

They noticed me! I shook a fist in the air. *You see that, Mother?*

I chose the farming division, with its week-long academic exam cycles once a month, and three standard years of practical training. And all along the way, there would be peers, and a few instructors, who never let me forget where I came from.

III.

"So, the pickup is in, what, twenty-three days?" I said.

"Twenty-three days," she echoed.

Five hundred and fifty-two hours. After that, the Ring would be too far out for us to reach.

Upon arrival, we were dropped off at the heliopause while the Ring continued her journey, skirting the outer fringes of the system in a great arc. Once our task was finished, we would rendezvous with the Ring on the other side of the heliopause as she made her way back into deep space.

"Twenty-three days," I muttered. There would be no rescue. "And it's a fourteen-day flight to the pickup point. So that's nine days. We must leave in nine days."

"More than enough time to effect repairs and try and save this cluster-fuck."

"Excuse me?"

"I'll begin the repairs. Karlyn, I want you to scrutinise the stored data that led up to the Platform crash and look for traces of a contaminant."

"You need to take a step back and get some perspective," I said.

"We don't pack up until we determine what went wrong. That's standard procedure."

"Under normal circumstances, I'd agree," I said, "but the circumstances are not normal. If I may remind the Senior, as things lie, emergency procedure supersedes all others. We're now in survival mode."

"I'm trying to save our professional asses here," she said. "Or does that not mean anything to you, Karlyn ano-Kerr?"

As senior bio-farmer and planetfall coordinator, the blame for losing the stock would fall squarely on her shoulders. I understood that; I could even empathise. But I would never put my life at risk. She shouldn't ask me to. She, as the Senior, should follow the correct procedure. After all, she had lived her whole life that way. We both had.

"And how are you going to accomplish that?" I said. "Without beams or comms we won't know of any course corrections the Ring will have to make over the next few days. We'd be flying blind."

"Stop being hysterical, Karlyn. Nine days is a solid safety margin."

"No, it isn't," I said, "and you know it. We have their last-known course and position up until a few minutes ago when those systems died. If we leave now, we can make a fairly strong estimate of where the Ring will be in twenty-three days, even if they perform a few course corrections, which they will. Our safety margin starts now. Every day, every hour we wait, raises the prospect the Ring will make more and more manoeuvres, so much so that our calculations will be way off the mark. We could miss the rendezvous by millions of kilometres. We won't have enough fuel to play catch-up."

"I'm still Senior here, Karlyn," she said. "Don't forget that."

"No one's coming to get us, Cruz."

"*Stop!*" She drew a measured breath, and her face

softened a little. "I hear you, Karlyn. Okay, I am open to compromise. If we can't determine what happened in three days, we leave. Will that satisfy you?"

I hesitated.

"I could order this," she said, "but I'd rather have a willing partner. We're talking about our positions—our professional lives! Help me, Karlyn. Help yourself."

My brain froze, and I couldn't think of anything to say.

She leaned into the camera. "You're not going to lie back and give up, are you?"

Cruz knew everything about me, of course. I'd been more open with Cruz than she'd ever been with me. And she knew the sweet spot, where to apply pressure, by invoking Mother Moira without ever mentioning her name.

"I suppose that could be enough time if we sleep in short bursts," I said. "The important part is seeing if I can authenticate the stock. As the grids are locked, I might be able to open them up with a direct interface. I'll go for a walk to the nodules ASAP."

"I'll get on those repairs," she said.

"Okay," I said. "Just going to drop by medical first. I can scrutinise the data on the crash from there."

"How badly are you hurt?"

I snorted. "Now you want to know?"

She frowned at me. "Fix yourself up and get to it."

"Three days, Cruz," I said and cut off the link.

IV.

I had met Cruz in training. She was a few years older than me. After a time, I discovered she was from a district two over from where I was born. Cruz had won the Junior Lottery, as I had—a victory, complete with silent benefactor. Those from our background never talked about that part. I suppose our silence was a way of dealing with the heated embarrassment that your future came from the hands of one who floated.

Going Above meant you got away from the unrelenting grind and the outbursts of social unrest. And you got away from the corruption, the local politicians who claimed to have your back but who were so easily bribed.

In Cruz, I had never seen someone so brazen, so cavalier, and all the while maintaining a determined focus to get the job done. It was that drive and energy that initially attracted me to her. At first, our conversations flowed naturally and our time together never seemed strained. But what I had admired about her was what eventually put a wedge between us.

She didn't like the slightest touch of chaos and could not handle a bit of spontaneity because it might jeopardise her success. She'd arranged her life and work in such a way that nothing should be unexpected because everything was well-ordered and in its place.

An incident like this must be killing her inside.

"Rerouting some of these systems may not be so easy," Cruz said.

I sat in medical, the Med AI going over my burns more thoroughly, when she called in and hit me with that little piece of her little mind.

I stared into the vid-cam. "You sounded positive a few hours ago."

She shrugged. "If you say so."

"We still have sixty hours. Haven't given up yet, have you?"

She narrowed her eyes, razor-sharp, and I grinned.

"Anyway," I added. "You said nothing about your doubts before."

Another shrug. "My way of keeping your morale up, I suppose."

"How sweet," I said flatly. "Didn't know you still cared."

"I haven't cared in a long time."

I would have called her on that but decided to leave it alone. Rejection was something she couldn't handle, so reminding her of it, of my decision to end it with her—well, no point in ripping open old wounds, no matter how much pleasure it would have given me to watch her explode.

"What's your med progress?" Cruz said.

"Had a few new skin patches weaved onto my more serious burns, which have taken hold nicely. And my new suit is ready." I removed it from the tank and pulled it on, watching the morning sunlight ooze its way through the winter foliage.

"Have fun out there," Cruz said.

The hint of sarcasm in her voice was not lost on me.

"Next time you should join me," I said, stalking through the lower deck to the equipment locker. My reinforced bones felt heavy inside me. "Watching you try and cope with full gravity would be a sight to behold."

"No thanks. I did my time as a groundside worker. Terrestrial mud crawling is not for me. The stench, the filth, bad working conditions—"

I frowned at the camera above me. "Where's your dedication to the stock?"

"Whose stock? Theirs or ours?"

"Last time I checked, there wasn't much of a difference."

She made a guttural sound in her throat.

"So, Cruz, you don't feel any connection to our siblings, groundside." Her unfounded air of superiority was another aspect of her attitude I found intolerable. "Ironic, don't you think?"

"How so?"

I caught her eyes in the vid and stared at her, hard. "Don't forget where you come from, Cruz."

"And where is that? We're the flowers of the wide-open spaces, Karlyn."

"What the fuck is that supposed to mean?" I said, digging through the locker.

"It means what it means."

I rolled my eyes. "Instead of spouting prosaic shit, why don't you get the data beams back online?"

"Why don't you run another diagnostic on the crash data?"

"I ran three, Cruz, all while I was getting patched up. There was nothing wrong with the equipment. No trace of any contamination yet, but it's got to be there. I'll look again after I get to the nodules."

"So, the equipment was fine," she said, then her voice turned cold, clinical. "That is, until you engaged the Platform's seeding protocols which crashed the system."

My ears burned.

"You'd better point that shit somewhere else, Cruz."

"Touchy, aren't we?"

"Are you suggesting I wasn't paying attention? That I did something wrong?" I was grinding my teeth. I grabbed my helmet and secured the locker.

She looked at me blankly. "I'm just saying what happened based on your own analysis. Up until the seeding protocols were employed, there were no technical issues. Don't you find that a bit curious?"

"I did my job, Cruz. And the protocols were green. Run a diagnostic on those yourself."

"I plan on it," she said.

"Knock yourself out."

She smirked. "Remember who you're talking to."

Yeah, the senior bio-farmer; the bio-tech phenomenon named Cruz des-Manas. Hallelujah.

She opened a tool kit and ran the fingers of one hand over a console. I heard the sound of an access panel clicking open.

"Got a timeframe on completing the repairs?" I asked.

"If you think you can do a better job, dearest, come on up. You're welcome to it."

I had no words for that—well, nothing suitable to avoid a full-on argument—so I said the most mundane thing I could think of: "See you on the uplift."

"Don't forget to wash when you're done."

It was her turn to cut the link.

V.

Sonic blade in hand, I slashed my way through the foliage toward the clearing and the organiform nodules the drones had set down. I'd landed two kilometres away from them. My external helmet mic was on, and as I walked, I heard small creatures scatter through the underbrush, while above, colourful birds spoke to each other in shrieks and wailing cries.

I was reminded of the floating arboretums of Above, with their colourful array of plant life and creatures—insects, birds, and other small animals—engineered for zero gravity. I would go there during the rest days between semesters to relax.

Cruz had been qualified for two standard years by the time my final academic year came around. During the long gaps between systems, she would have time to come see me. We would let the serenity of the gardens wash away the pressures on us to constantly prove ourselves. And to reconnect.

And it was in the arboretum, on one particular day, that I decided I needed to go back Below. For no reason I could explain, I was overwhelmed with the need to see the place and the people who'd cared for me, and to hold the canister that contained Mother's ashes...

I could see the clearing and the plain where the nodules sat in their berths. The instant I stepped out from between the closely packed trees something loomed over me, and I jumped back. I looked up.

The Beta habitat, or something resembling it, had regrown and sprung up during the night like a wild grouping of vines, twisted and interlocking. Filaments resembling veins wandered out across the smooth areas of lattices and giant leafy enclosures. It was massive and still growing, fibres breaking through the soil across the plain, reaching up toward the sun. Despite the mutations,

I imagined the Platform would still meet its pre-programmed size of fifty-three square kilometres.

My comms chimed.

Before I knew what I was doing, I approached the part of the habitat nearest me, hand outstretched, rubbing the lattices and snaking branches. The giant leaves were translucent with a light green tinge, and I could see through to where the nodules sat in their mouldings, thousands of them, undisturbed. Each one was a pip seven-point-five centimetres in diameter. Rows and rows of life-bearing, human seeds.

My comms rattled.

I had never seen anything like it. The sequencers had fail-safe coding to prevent virus proliferation when drawing upon alien ecosystems to grow the human stock and their habitats; coding that instantly recognised a virus upon infection and quickly put cells into a state of viral resistance. Hyper-aggressive anti-viral proteins then prevented virus replication.

As a result of the fail-safes, the only modifications made to the stock would be by the Platform itself, small alterations so that our groundside siblings could live comfortably in their new environment. Sometimes that would be large, protruding noses to warm and humidify cold, dry air on worlds of snow-capped mountains and icy tundra; or an increase in bone density for heavy gravity worlds; or in the case of protein incompatibility, where native proteins and sugars are found to be right-handed instead of left-handed, adapting the human stock so they could draw nutrients eating what the land provided.

For this world, the day and night cycle was twenty-four hours exactly, and the daytime temperature hardly ever rose above zero Celsius in winter and nineteen in the summer. Pressure? One atmosphere. All in all, nothing that would suggest the need for modifications. The stock would grow as sequenced and, when ready, leave the relative security of the Platform domes to inhabit the world around them. It was textbook. Or it was supposed to be.

I knew then this was not the by-product of a contaminant. A contaminant would not cause extensive mutations like these. Contaminants destroyed, outright.

My comms clanged for my attention.

VI.

When I applied for and was given leave to go Below, Cruz didn't apply to come with me, even though as my partner she could have. Though we were between worlds, between systems, she came up with some work-related excuse and disappeared for a few days. I don't know why this surprised me, but I was deeply hurt. And offended.

Cruz had never gone back. Not since I'd known her. When I asked her to come with me, she recoiled. "Why would I do that?" she'd said, clearly not expecting an answer.

"Maybe you'd like to accompany me, for fuck's sake," I replied. "It's what partners do, isn't it?"

Cruz said nothing.

*

"Where the hell have you been?" Cruz said. "I know your comms are working."

"I'm kind of busy here."

"When I call you, it's for a fucking good reason," she snapped. "Don't leave me in limbo like that again."

I sighed. "What is it, Cruz?"

She clicked her tongue. "Not long ago, I started receiving a strange pulsing over Beta's channel."

"So did I. And I'm inside it right now."

"Inside what?"

"The Platform, rather the gestation structure. She's up and running, though deformed."

"Why isn't your cam on?"

I adjusted my suit's camera eye and linked up. "See that?"

Cruz was unusually quiet.

"I've been plugged into the grids for a long time now," I said, "but I've been getting no data from it. Something's blocking me at every turn. Whatever's happened here, there's no way to tell if the coding in the nodules has been compromised. The only way to find out is to reactivate the protocols. They seem to be working now, I got a green light again."

"And that's exactly what we're *not* going to do," she said. "If the mutations we're seeing to get into the nodules, if we allow the stock to gestate, to grow—"

"I didn't say I was going to reactivate it, did I? I only said we could. I need to figure out what's blocking me, then I can get the data we need to determine what's happened."

"You don't have time," she said. "We need to go, Karlyn. Now."

You do not get close to a person without being able to read them, to pick up on subtlety—tone of voice, an imperceptible movement of head or hand, a fleeting expression...

"We still have twenty-two hours," I said. "What's going on?"

"Changed my mind," she said. "Senior's prerogative. I've already linked into the bug's systems and prepped her for uplift, so you'd better start back."

"Cruz," I said. "I know I was obstinate before, about staying here, but I think I can figure this out."

"You've spent thirty-eight hours trying to figure it out, and you still got nothing."

That was a sudden slap to the face.

"Now's not the time to take potshots at my skill set," I snapped. "So, what's happening with the long-range comms? Or the data beam?"

"Nothing," she said. "There's too much damage to those core systems."

I went cold. It would not take thirty-eight hours to figure out those systems were irreparably damaged. She would have known that while I sat in medical.

"You knew all along," I said, "and you didn't think it worth mentioning? What the fuck have you been doing all this time?"

"Running additional diagnostics on the Platform's data feed before the crash, among other things," she said. "We're finished, Karlyn. I'm finished. Get back up here. We're leaving."

"Cruz—"

"I didn't order you before," she said, "but I'm ordering you now. Stop what you're doing and get up here."

VII.

The bug flew—a bumpy ride, and not unexpected, considering the damage; some of the systems were still a bit touchy. What was unexpected was that I lost all power one thousand kilometres from the surface. I was fifty kilometres out from the command shuttle.

There was no returning to the surface now.

Using my EVA suit, I left the bug and closed the remaining distance. I cycled through an airlock and tore off the suit, throwing each piece of it against a bulkhead for good measure.

*

After storming through the corridors, I entered the cockpit, but Cruz was not there. I opened a ship-wide comm link and called her name. She responded by voice only. The vid feed at her location was down.

"Cruz, I can't see you."

"I've just left the service crawlspace in engineering," she said. "Had to check that flutter in the main drive system again. She'll be fine to fly. The estimated coordinates for the Ring's location are already in the Nav systems. Auto-Nav is engaged. She'll break orbit in eight minutes."

"The bug's dead," I said.

"I know. We can't spare the fuel to retrieve it and I'm

not sure you could repair it alone if we did. I'm just glad you made it."

Taking pot-shots at my skills again. My head swam with hot fury. Against my better judgement, I had agreed to stay groundside, but then I found I was making progress; I was sure of it. I might salvage the situation, after all.

Everything was always about her, what she needed, what she wanted, and how she planned to get it. But hiding information, this quick about-face and the urgency to get me back up here, made no sense.

"I want an explanation," I barked.

"Okay," she said. "What crashed the Platform was not a technical error. We've both done enough diagnostics on the data to establish that. And while you were out, I did additional checks and found no traces of a contaminant. I know you've come to the same conclusion, so we can rule out your proposed saboteur. What brought the whole thing down came from *outside*."

That caught me off guard.

"That's what the fail-safes are for," I said, "to stop invasive viruses, to prevent unwanted mutations."

"Apparently, this one can get past the filters. My guess is it's a latent paragene, carrying dormant instructions."

Okay, so a small, independently replicating piece of extrachromosomal cytoplasmic DNA can be transferred from one organism to another, carrying at least one gene beneficial to the host organism. Nothing usual there. Paragenes are one part of the myriad processes in establishing and growing the Platform and the stock, groundside. That's Biology 101. What pricked my mind was the word "latent".

"And whatever those instructions are," she continued, "they're able to get through the filters as long as they stay dormant."

I thought of the Platform, and how it redesigned itself. "Are you sure?"

She scoffed. "Of course not. It's my theory. We don't have any data yet to prove it, but I'm fairly certain I'm right."

"What triggered them?"

"That's the question," she said. "A question that could take more time than we have to answer. Karlyn, you can't break into the grids. That's not a reflection of your abilities. Maybe if you had more time, a few weeks, a month, maybe you'd get in. But that's a big maybe. The truth is, we don't know what we're dealing with here, and we don't have the time to figure it out."

I'd never heard her sound so lost, so repentant, so broken. And so honest. She'd put all her life and focus into her ambitions so that her place among those Above would stand unquestioned. It was all she'd ever wanted.

At that moment, I can honestly say my heart broke for her.

"So, you lied about the damage," I said. "To buy time to try and salvage your position. Without knowing what was really going on down there, that's one hell of a risk to take."

"Me, taking risks?" She laughed sourly. "How about that?" I could sense a change in her, an air of dour acceptance. "I know you understand what it takes for one of us to get as far as we have, Karlyn."

Of course, I understood. I had felt the pressure to prove my worth to those who saw nothing in me. And in that moment I knew that Mother Moira felt it, too. In my own way, for good or for bad, I had become her, her dreams, her yearnings of opportunities lost, yearnings made manifest in my flesh.

I did not know what additional pressures drove Cruz so forcibly. We never spoke about her past, about her life before she was lifted Above, and so these were things I would never know, things that would remain as mysterious as the universe itself. Things that would shape her as a whole person and produce those qualities in her that would eventually drive me away.

Above.

Below.

Us and Them.

What a mindfuck.

"Cruz," I said. "What happened here is not your fault."

She snorted. "We have no time to gather data, no explanation for what happened. You know they'll have to blame someone. If I was born Above, I might draw a reprimand and get sidelined for promotion. As a resident from Below, well, it'll be me and three judges in a closed courtroom. I'll be stripped of everything. Sent back."

I felt sick in my gut.

"I gave my soul to get here," she said. "Dedicated my life to those Above, and at the first sign of trouble they'll turn on me. Know why? Because we're flotsam, Karlyn. I'm flotsam."

I didn't know what to say, but she was right.

"And you know what?" she growled. "My failure here will simply reinforce the thinking that underpins every shitty little thing they believe about us. Well, I won't be a scapegoat. I won't give them the satisfaction."

I heard the chiming of a control panel being touched.

"You'll survive all this, Karlyn," she said, "but I'm the responsible officer here. Accountability rests with me. You'll simply get bumped off the team and relegated to a lower post. Maybe you could start over, live another life. Me? This *is* my life. I built it with my own two hands, and it's *mine*."

And then it finally hit me: *I'm not sure you could repair it alone...*

"Cruz," I said, slowly, deliberately. "Why can't I see you?"

"Believe me, it's better this way."

I heard the hiss of a door sealing shut.

"Cruz, what are you doing?" Stupid question. I knew what she was doing. I frantically glanced across the panel to my left. "I can't see the status of airlock four."

"That's because I've disabled it."

"Whoa, whoa, whoa, Cruz, hang on!"

"Three minutes to departure," she said.

An alarm sounded, pulsing through the comm. My fingers danced across the panel, trying to reroute the controls for the airlock, though it was fruitless. She had locked me out of the auto-Nav, too. It wouldn't give me back control until the departure sequence was completed and the shuttle was underway. If Cruz was anything, she was thorough.

"Cruz don't do this. Just talk to me." My throat filled with the ragged overtones of hysteria. "For once in your damned life, *talk* to me!"

The alarm became a steady note.

"Cruz, you don't even know if your theory about latent paragenes is what's happened here. You said yourself, we don't have any data."

"You saw the Platform. It's the only thing that makes sense. And hey," she added, with more tenderness than I had ever thought her voice could carry. "Remember who you're talking to."

Hot tears cut tracks down my face.

"When the outer door blows open," she said, "you won't need to correct for any minor changes made in the shuttle's position to stay on target for rendezvous. Air pressure, force of decompression, it's all factored into my numbers."

Of course it was.

"Stop, Cruz, *please!*"

"One minute to departure."

"You single-minded, phlegmatic, stubborn bitch!" I cried. "You always were insufferable. You know that?"

"Yeah," she said. "Tell me something new."

I wiped my face with both hands.

"Karlyn," she said. "Don't forget where you come from. Not ever. Don't forget—"

A shudder rippled through the ship, and the alarm went dead.

VIII.

There's nothing more about Cruz that I could say that I haven't already said; no other words I could use to describe her than those already used. But I will say this, they didn't deserve her. They didn't deserve any of us. Those floaters Above, the Zero-G Apostles. Condescending, derisive, and detached from those things that bound us together—the respect of a common ancestry.

We had spent our lives fighting and pushing and proving we had a right to our place Above. But you can't earn what others are unwilling to give.

Mother Moira knew this all too well...

*

While I was still within range, I pulled on my digivisor and tapped into Beta Platform. I keyed in the final coding sequence and engaged the seeding protocols. At first, the algorithms scattered, then fell into place, piece by piece, creating a pattern both familiar and new.

I don't know why I did it. Without any studies, I had no idea what the stock would become. Maybe in some strange way, I wanted to pay homage to Cruz. In my mind, I made her out to be the Mother of a new, enigmatic species, one that would live a life more worthy than any of us.

Or maybe I did it out of spite, to shake my fist at those Above who would sneer at us.

Maybe it didn't matter.

I turned the heating down throughout the shuttle, just enough for ice to form on the inside of the windows, making the view outside hazy and unclear. I stripped off my suit. I wanted the frigid air to prick my skin. I needed the edge it would give me to stay sharp, to feel alive...

I studied the numbers in the Nav systems as they rolled up the screen. Of course, Cruz was the Senior and the more experienced in such things. An expert. But without long-range comms or the data beam, even Cruz couldn't guarantee the number of course corrections the Ring would've made and was making at that very moment, or if it would be anywhere near where she was sending me.

I didn't know if I would make it back.

Maybe that didn't matter, either.

What did matter—the one unassailable truth—was that Cruz had done her best under the circumstances, and that was enough for me.

ACKNOWLEDGEMENTS

"Heart of the City, Heart of the Sea" first appeared in *BFS Horizons* magazine, issue 11, and reprinted in the *Portals, Gateways and Doors* anthology, published by Farthest Star Publishing. "The Roots of Love" first appeared in *BFS Horizons* magazine, issue 14. "What Happened to Mrs Eleonora Valdemar, Discovered in a Series of Diary Entries" first appeared in the Fox Spirit anthology *American Monsters, Part Two*, under the title "What Happened to Mrs Eleonora Valdemar", and reprinted in *Short Story America, Volume Seven* and *Masque & Maelström: The Reluctant Exhumation of Edgar Allan Poe*, published by JayHenge Publishing. "Children of Itzamná" first appeared in *Speculative City* magazine. "Song for the Asking" first appeared in *Stories for Chip: A Tribute to Samuel R Delany*, published by Rosarium Press. "Slipping Sideways" first appeared in *Rocket Science: Science Fiction and Fact* and later reprinted in *Everyone: Worlds Without Walls*, published by Starship Sofa. "The Clarity of Ice" first appeared in *Zama Shorts* as a stand-alone, short story e-book. "The Stars Must Wait," is The Science Fiction and Fantasy South Africa's Nova winning story for 2024 and appeared in *Probe SF* magazine.

ABOUT THE AUTHOR

Carmelo Rafalà comes from a large Sicilian family. He completed his MA in Comparative English Literature at the University of South Africa, followed by an MSC at Central Connecticut State University, and a teaching qualification from the University of Sussex. His fiction has appeared in various anthologies and his novella, *The Madness of Pursuit*, is published by Guardbridge Books. He is the Science Fiction and Fantasy South Africa 2024 winner for his story "The Stars Must Wait". He lives on the south coast of England.

More Intriguing Fiction from Guardbridge Books.

The Madness Of Pursuit
by Carmelo Rafalà

Dema Ägan is a notorious pirate woman, who killed her former captain, stole his ship, and plies the seas with her J'Niah witch lover, Rymah. Or so the legends say.

As this adventure – on seas filled with danger, ancient power, love and betrayal – unfolds from multiple viewpoints, we come to see there might be more to her story than commonly believed.

Off The Beaten Path
by Gustavo Bondoni

22 science fiction and fantasy stories by the award winning Argentinian author. Includes two new, never before published pieces. Set in corners of the world oft ignored: from the Namib desert, to the Amazon rainforest, from Tierra del Fuego, to the far side of the moon.

When you dare step Off the Beaten Path the results could be catastrophic but the rewards could be great.

Soul Searching
by Stephen Embleton

South African police use a device that can track souls in a harrowing search for a serial killer. But when one's soul can incriminate them before birth, can there be justice?
NOMMO Awards Best Novel 2020 Finalist.

All are available at our website and online retailers.
http://guardbridgebooks.co.uk

www.ingramcontent.com/pod-product-compliance
Ingram Content Group UK Ltd.
Pitfield, Milton Keynes, MK11 3LW, UK
UKHW041918011125
8712UKWH00002B/170

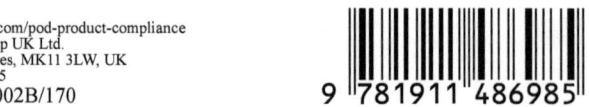